MW00366230

PRAISE FOR

DEEMER'S INLET

BY STEPHEN BURDICK

"With wit and humanity, Chief Eldon Quick faces a series of gruesome killings among a handful of characters, some who make his job harder, some easier, but people aren't always who they seem to be. Capturing life in a small beach town on Florida's Gulf Coast, Burdick brings an engaging new voice to this swift and gritty crime story—one that will keep you guessing."

> —**Jeffery Hess**, author of *Beachhead*, *Tushhog*,
> and *No Salvation*

"Deemer's Inlet—a sleepy coastal town woken wide awake by a serial killer with a pocketful of matches. From the flames leaping sky-high on the first page to the tight, satisfying conclusion, Burdick keeps the pace and pulse pounding. Deemer's Inlet is classic crime writing at its best."

> —**Steph Post**, author of *Lightwood*

"Serial arson becomes serial murder becomes a bewildering game of cat and mouse. Burdick's Eldon Quick uncovers a criminal cabal in his sleepy town of Deemer's Inlet."

> —**David Tromblay**, author of *As You Were* and **Sangre Road**

IN A SLEEPY SEASIDE TOWN

DEEMER'S INLET

MURDER IS WIDE AWAKE

STEPHEN BURDICK

SHOTGUN HONEY
2020

DEEMER'S INLET
Text copyright © 2020 Stephen Burdick

Published by Shotgun Honey, an imprint of Down & Out Books.

Shotgun Honey
215 Loma Road
Charleston, WV 25314
www.ShotgunHoney.com

Down & Out Books
3959 Van Dyke Rd, Ste. 265
Lutz, FL 33558
www.DownAndOutBooks.com

Cover Design by Bad Fido.

First Printing 2020.

ISBN-10: 1-64396-104-7
ISBN-13: 978-1-64396-104-0

For Debby Laramee, Kitty Smith,
and Maggie Cinnella.

You believed from the beginning.

DEEMER'S INLET

Stephen Burdick

··ONE··

FLAMES ENGULFED TWO BOATS, and the charred remains of a third vessel smoldered just above the water line when I arrived at the Oyster Point dock. Firefighters were doing their best to battle the blaze, but an undersized parking lot compounded an already dangerous situation. The chance of an exploding fuel tank was a constant concern as they boldly inched closer to the inferno.

The onlookers scattered along the perimeter of the parking lot were nuisance enough, but the cars slowing to view the commotion were creating chaos. Most of Gulf Boulevard is a four-lane road. It narrows to two lanes along this patch of coastline, putting undue pressure on my patrolmen to keep the traffic moving.

During a lull one of my men, Bo Simpson, ambled over to where my SUV was blocking all but a slight avenue of entry to the parking lot. "This isn't good, Chief. This isn't good at all."

"No, it isn't, Bo. I don't think they're going to get to those boats in time."

"We're gonna be in deep trouble if one of those babies blows up."

We watched the firefighters edge forward, gaining ground but losing time.

Sergeant Barney Andrews hustled up to us.

"Do you smell what I smell?" I said

"Yep, smells like gasoline, Chief."

Bo looked at Barney then at me. "You mean somebody did this on purpose?"

"The nose knows. No guarantee, of course."

Bo shook his head. "Oh, man, here comes another line of cars!"

He and Barney hurried back to Gulf Boulevard while I stayed in the parking lot and watched the overwhelming flames.

I listened to the crackling and popping, hoping I was wrong. Not about smelling gasoline, but about arson. Two times in as many weeks we'd dealt with a fire—two times too many for our little town. If *sleepy* is an appropriate description for any community, then it's perfect for Deemer's Inlet.

The most excitement I'd seen in my seven years on the job was a three-car accident that blocked Gulf Boulevard for the better half of a day. Now, two fires would be the topic at many breakfast tables—and at Town Hall. I shuddered to think of the number of people who would be bending my ear in the days to come. Not to mention the public scrutiny of my staff and me.

My thoughts were interrupted by a familiar and aggravating voice.

"Why didn't you call me, El?" Mayor Sam Hackney lost steam when he noticed my hardened expression, but quickly started in on me again. "I should have been contacted immediately!"

I hated his calling me "El." My name is Eldon, Eldon Quick.

"Sam, everything possible is being done. With all due respect, how is your being here helping matters?"

"I'm the mayor! It's my duty to be here for those burdened by tragedy. And it's your duty to call me when these unfortunate events occur."

Save the speeches, Sam. It's not an election year, I thought. "I'm sorry. I had other things on my mind."

"Well, next time, try to remember!"

"Hopefully, there won't be a *next time.*"

"What? Oh, yes, of course. Just don't forget who's in charge here."

Being a retired business administrator for some corporation in Michigan, Sam saw our town as the perfect vehicle to continue his self-proclaimed expertise in managing, I suspect. And since no one else wanted the job, he was elected to the position.

"Where do we stand, El? Did anyone get hurt? What about property damage? I see two boats on fire."

"Indian Rocks Fire got here as soon as they could. A third boat has been destroyed and is underwater over there. I'm guessing the others will be totaled. As for injuries, I haven't seen anyone down. See that ambulance parked over there? They haven't moved since they got here."

Sam glanced to his left and eyed the firefighters. "This is terrible. That dock's gonna cost me a fortune. Where are the boat owners? Do you know if they're here?"

Figures you're worried about the dock since you own it, I thought. "I have no idea. That's your department, isn't it?"

3

"Yes, of course. I must locate them right away. Keep me informed, El."

He bustled off to search the crowd.

"Jesus," I muttered.

"Yeah, it's a mess all right."

I turned to discover a grim-looking firefighter standing next to me.

"Chief, I'm Lieutenant Mike O'Malley." He removed his glove and extended his right hand.

"Wish it could have been under better circumstances, Lieutenant."

"More than you know, Chief."

"What do you mean?"

"One of my men spotted a woman down on the far end of the seawall. The ambulance team just got to her…and it's not looking good."

Through the open patches of billowing smoke, I saw the EMTs kneeling beside her with flashlights. I saw something else that made my heart sink. The woman was covered with a blanket.

"I'd better get over there," I said.

I rounded the fire trucks and moved to the small patch of grass where the woman fell. I could tell by the faces on the ambulance team it was too late.

"I guess I don't have to ask."

The EMT's face told me she'd experienced this kind of tragedy far too often.

"She's gone, Chief. She was dead before we got here."

"Was she burned or was it smoke inhalation?"

The lead EMT glanced at her partner. "You'd better have a look for yourself."

The victim bore the signs of a woman who'd led a rough life. A deeply tanned face held lines of premature aging. Scars showed clearly on her chin and cheek. What her face and clothes didn't show was any after-effects of burning or smoke.

"Good lord, her throat's been cut!"

"It was the first thing we noticed, Chief."

The wound was deep and vicious. Blood lost on her yellow t-shirt appeared as a dark red bib.

I quickly ran my eyes over the body. "She hasn't been dead very long. Rigor hasn't set in yet." I glanced over my shoulder at the crowd of gawkers. *The killer might still be here*. I turned back to the EMTs. "Cover her up. I'll call a forensics team."

"Chief, we were called to the motel fire last week. The gunshot wounds on that guy were fresh, too. We passed that information along to one of your patrolmen."

I nodded. "Yes, he told me, and I would appreciate your keeping a lid on it. Stick around, okay. I may need to talk to you later."

"Whatever we can do."

Arson and murder...not once, but twice, I thought. *How bizarre.*

In all my years in law enforcement, I'd never come across a situation like this, and certainly not twice in such a short period of time. I'd witnessed arson as an attempt to hide a murder, and arson as the cause of a murder, but never the combination of separate acts.

I studied the burning dock then looked back at the dead woman. *Was she killed before or during the fire? And why was she killed?*

The vessels moored along this stretch of backwater were commercial fishing boats. To be near a channel opening into the Gulf of Mexico, they were grouped together here. The docks had stood for decades. And while a certain amount of trouble always existed among the fisherman, nothing close to this kind of mayhem ever occurred.

Was she the arsonist, discovered and killed by one of the deck hands? Or did the arsonist kill her? I wondered. *Or was it something else?*

"Hey, what's going on here? I thought you said nobody was hurt!" Sam shouted as he walked toward us.

"Oh, Jesus, this is all I need," I mumbled.

The EMTs looked at one another.

"Why are you people standing around? Why aren't you doing something to—" Sam froze when he saw the blanket-covered body. "Oh, my god!"

"Sam, keep your voice down!"

"Is he dead?"

"No, *she's* dead, and the world doesn't need to know." I pulled my cell phone from my pants pocket. "I'm calling Forensics right now."

"Forensics! You mean she was—"

"Sam, if you don't shut up, I'm going to have them strap you to a stretcher and haul you outta here!"

"You can't talk to me like that! I'm the mayor! I can have you—"

"Right now you're nothing but a pain in my ass! *And* you're interfering with a criminal investigation! Now, if you don't be quiet, I'm going to arrest you!"

With the veins standing out on his forehead, Sam gritted his teeth and stormed off.

I attempted to restrain my anger by shifting my thoughts to the man found during the first fire a week ago.

James Mullen—nicknamed Mullet—was discovered a

short distance from the burning motel. Initially, I thought his death and the fire to be unrelated. The autopsy determined he died around the same time, an unusual situation, but not so much as to prove a connection.

Mullet worked the fishing boats. When he wasn't working, he found ways of getting into trouble. Drunk and disorderly, assault, theft, you name it, and there you'd find him.

I'd assumed someone had grown tired of his act and put an end to it. Now, I wasn't so sure.

When Forensics arrived, an unofficial assessment determined the woman, identity still unknown, had died where she lay. They found no signs of a struggle *or* a murder weapon. Until the Fire Marshal completed his investigation, I would have to treat each incident as separate, and not related. Call it a hunch or gut feeling, but something about the two killings put me on edge.

I left the docks a little after midnight and went to the office. Home in bed is where I should have been, but I wanted to go over Mullen's file first.

At this time of morning I would be the sole inhabitant of the small room designated for the police department. Lined with filing cabinets, an administrative assistant's desk, and an undersized holding cell, the room barely fit the requirements of the force.

I moved easily through the darkness to my office, turned on the lights, and sat down at my desk. Sitting atop a pile of papers was the Mullen file.

In one sense, the murders were eerily similar. Both victims were found during a fire. Neither was a person of note or wealth. Mullet was a fisherman. The dead woman looked as though she could have been. The kill methods were different, but done with stealth and precision. Two closely spaced bullets to the chest ended the fisherman's life. A clean cut severing the jugular eliminated the woman, who bled out quickly.

I wonder if they knew each other. Maybe they wanted in on some illegal activity. Or maybe they wanted out.

I'm not a big believer in coincidence, but I don't discount it. *My* thinking is more linear. Things happen for a reason.

At first the motel fire was written off as an electrical problem. Built in the 1950's, The Happy Clam offered a mom-and-pop setting to those desiring serenity by the shore. Its ancient wiring *would* be suspect. But the Fire Marshal determined arson to be the cause, undoing the easy theory.

When I had called the absentee owner in Pennsylvania, I was surprised by his reaction. Although relieved there were no fatalities, he expressed regret that the structure wasn't completely destroyed. I guess the insurance pay-out was more attractive than the hassle and cost of repair.

So here I sat in my office about to put on my detective's hat to do the investigation myself. Our little police department isn't budgeted for a detective, and I didn't want to bring in another agency. Outside assistance wasn't necessary in the past, so why bother with it now?

The job done on Mullen looked like a professional hit. I'd seen the work of assassins in my previous stint as a detective on the east coast of south Florida. In Miami, there was a wide variety of ways to dispose of people. A small caliber weapon, usually a .22, made quick work of a mark. Such was the case with Mullen.

I came to the same conclusion when I first saw the woman.

A surprise attack most likely left her incapacitated and choking. That is, I assumed it to be a surprise attack. Most people don't willingly stand by while their throats are being cut. And since there were no signs of a struggle, it seemed to follow. The next question? Who did she piss off to warrant being killed? My focus was broken when I heard the front door open.

The lights to the outer office came on, and Martha Bevins appeared in my doorway.

"Good morning, Eldon. You're in early today."

"Good morning, Marty. Actually, I'm in here late today."

Marty's official title was Administrative Assistant/ Dispatcher, but she did practically everything around the office. Her father was a cop, and, most recently, chief. His passing was the reason I came to Deemer's Inlet. Marty had a pleasant way about her. When she was right, she didn't rub it in your face. When she was wrong, she admitted it. *And* we had something in common.

"Martha makes me sound like a grandmother," she once grumbled.

My name—Eldon—didn't set well with me, either. And coupled with my last name Quick—was a source of great torment during my school years.

"Eldon Quick? No, Eldon Slow."

My classmates were right. Plodding, lumbering, and Neanderthal more aptly described my attempts at moving faster than a walk.

"I heard about the fire," Marty said. "I guess you were up all night and didn't get much sleep."

"You're right. Unfortunately, a woman was murdered, so I hung around until Forensics was done."

"Another murder? Oh, no. What happened?"

"I don't know. I'll have to wait for the Medical Examiner's report."

"How was she killed?"

"Her throat was cut."

Marty made a face. "Yuck!" She paused a moment then caught herself. "Want some coffee, Eldon?"

"Thanks, I could use some."

I often wondered why Marty never became a cop. She had the brains for it, and seeing as how her father's life was devoted to law enforcement, it only seemed natural that she would follow suit. Maybe her current position was enough for her.

I drifted back into thought, only to be interrupted again.

"Good morning, Chief."

I looked up and discovered Charlie Bates and Reed Logan filling the doorway.

"Good morning, fellas."

"Anything special we need to do today?" Charlie asked.

"Nothing comes to mind. Oh, did you happen to notice if they fixed the pothole on Scallop Drive?"

"Yep, all patched nice and neat."

"Good, that'll put an end to Sam Hackney's hourly phone calls. I still haven't figured out why he calls *me*."

Charlie and Reed laughed.

"How bad was the fire?" Reed asked.

"Three boats lost, and about half the dock."

Marty slid between them and set my coffee on the desk. "Here you go."

"Would you like me to make sure the crime scene is still secure? I mean, where they found the body?" Reed asked.

"How did you find out about that?" I said.

"Gloria Hackney. I ran into her at Suzie's Cafe."

"Yeah, she said the woman was cut to ribbons," Charlie said.

I winced and closed my eyes.

It was debatable as to who had the bigger mouth—the mayor or his wife.

"Just make sure the barricade tape is still up, and no one is poking around."

"Will do, Chief," Reed said.

Charlie nodded; Reed saluted.

They left as discreetly as they had arrived.

Charlie had been on the force as long as Barney and Bo. Reed was a rookie, eager and ambitious, but a likeable kid. With an unflappable professional demeanor, he always looked like his uniform was pressed twice a day.

"Marty, when Barney gets in, tell him I need to see him."

She smiled and saluted. "Will do, Chief."

"Get outta here."

A vision of the unknown woman's wound popped into my mind along with another disturbing thought. What if a serial killer had wandered into our town? Two murders and gone would make for an ugly headline. And that was the last thing I needed.

Although not on any maps promoting vacation getaways, our little town had its fair share of winter visitors. They were the kind of folks who enjoyed a quiet retreat, not the glitz and glamour of a Fort Lauderdale or Miami Beach. Word of a killer on the loose would hurt the local businesses, not to mention casting a shadow over the community. And I would be the one called on the carpet to explain why the problem had yet to be resolved.

Worse still would be if the killer resided here, hiding in plain sight. With flapping jaws like Sam and Gloria, he would know every move we made. Apprehending him would be extremely difficult.

No, we have two isolated incidents with commonalities, I assured myself.

I couldn't add to an already difficult task by injecting speculation. Too many theories invited confusion. Too few brought the risk of oversight. Play it as it lies was the way to do it. A knock on the door interrupted me again.

"You wanted ta see me, Chief?"

"Yeah, Barney, come on in." I waited for him to be seated. "Look, I'm going to have to bow out this Sunday. I've got to get a handle on this latest murder."

His face drew into disappointment. "Sorry ta hear that. Do ya really think there's a connection b'tween the two?"

Looking at the man, one might think Barney just a good old boy barely able to keep from tripping over himself. His personality and flat talking wouldn't deceive anyone into believing he was a mental giant. He possessed a unique quality, though. He had a mysterious knack for reasoning his way to the answer by using simple methods. *Country Smart*, I called it. And, like me, he loved to fish.

"Barney, sometimes you amaze me. Are you a mind reader or something?"

He grinned and tucked his thumbs inside his gun belt. "Naw, Chief, I figger it this a-way. We found ol' Mullet after the Happy Clam fire last week. We found that woman durin' the fire last night. Did the same feller do it? Maybe no, maybe so. If I's you, I'd be thinking the same thing."

I smiled and shook my head. "You know I'd give you a promotion if I could."

"Thanks, Chief, but I like bein' a sergeant. I'm kinda dug in like a Alabama tick, ya know."

"Really? *Lieutenant* Barney Andrews has a nice ring to it."

"Naw, them shiny bars on muh shirt would make me nervous. B'sides, I'd hafta start makin' decisions insteada just doin' muh job."

"All right, if you say so. You look tired. Go home and get some sleep."

"Sure thing, Chief. But if ya need me, just holler."

Barney may have fooled other folks, but he didn't fool me. When it came to making decisions, he grabbed the bull by the horns. I'd heard the gossip, making it sound as if I carried him because we were fishing buddies. In reality, Barney helped the department more than he hurt it. He just didn't care to stand front and center.

I had a good group of people around me and wanted to keep it that way. A powerful feeling told me I needed every one of them now more than ever.

· · TWO · ·

THE REST OF THE MORNING came and went without further incident. Not to say we didn't have our normal assortment of mishaps.

A fender bender around nine-thirty inconvenienced motorists on Gulf Boulevard for an hour. Charlie and Reed saw to it right away and took control of the situation.

Our resident feuding families held their weekly shouting match, but Reed defused the skirmish in a timely manner. For a young fellow, he has an inordinate amount of patience. He once told me, "The trick is to keep them out of jail," quite a different philosophy than his adrenaline-charged peers.

The competence of my staff made it easy for me to concentrate on more pressing matters.

I'd resigned myself to the belief that I wouldn't receive the Medical Examiner's report for a few days. Other communities and high-profile cases received preferential treatment. Our little village didn't rank as high on their to do list. On a positive note, it gave me some much-needed time to mull over my problem.

Theorizing both fires to be a diversion for the murders, I supposed the killer to be one and the same, and skilled in the art of elimination. These were not some knee-jerk reactions. His method was deceptive, neat, and efficient.

In the case of the Happy Clam fire, he'd pulled off a remarkable feat by accomplishing

his goal in the evening. At a time when people might be checking in or walking the beach, he'd managed to kill a man and start a fire without being seen.

The same was true of the second fire.

Barney had called me shortly after 10 p.m., and by 10:20 the Indian Rocks Beach Fire Department arrived. The Oyster Point docks were not that far from Gulf Boulevard and easily seen by passing vehicles. They were basically deserted at night, but activity on and around the boats could go on until morning.

I had to tip my hat to his boldness. Granted, committing murder is easier than robbing a bank, but to do so in the open took brass.

Around noon I started to feel the effects of my all-night vigil.

"Eldon? Eldon, wake up."

For a moment I thought I was home in Hialeah with my wife. I opened my eyes to find Marty standing beside my desk wearing a huge smile.

"Oh, I must have dozed off."

"Sorry to wake you, but the M.E.'s report just arrived."

I rubbed a hand over my face. "That was quick. Must be a slow day."

Her smile took on a look of sentiment. "My father

used to take cat-naps at his desk. He'd get so embarrassed when I caught him."

"Well, I'm not embarrassed. I'm tired."

"I know." She handed me the report. "Forensics sent over the prints earlier, so I ran them through the system."

I lowered my eyes to the report. "And?"

"Lucille Jean Jarvis, forty-six, no home address, and no occupation. Last held a job in 1998. She has a record of drug possession and prostitution."

"So it's safe to say we can rule out robbery as a motive."

"Eldon, could she have worked on the boats like Mullet?"

"From what I saw of her, I would say it's a distinct possibility." I glanced at the Medical Examiner's report. "Scars on her left cheek and chin, and numerous scars on her hands. She was probably a fish cutter."

Marty pinched her face into a puzzled scowl. "Why those two? We're not talking about people with any money."

"Maybe they were in the wrong place at the wrong time. Or maybe they saw something incriminating."

"What about the fires? Were they set to draw attention away from the murders?"

"Maybe. Or maybe the victims saw the arsonist."

"Hmm…that seems unusual. Arsonists get off on setting fires, not murder. But, I suppose if he's caught in the act…still, getting caught twice seems like poor planning. Why not wait until the middle of the night to set the next fire?"

I would never make light of the variety of expressions on Marty's face when she was attempting to understand the criminal mind. She'd cock her head to the right, accent details with her eyes, and ramble on in a one-sided conversation.

"Your guess is as good as mine."

I didn't want to get into the profile of a serial killer. Marty knew as well as anyone that their primary targets were women and children. The satisfaction came from power and control. This killer thought out his plan of attack.

There was another possibility to be considered. Sociopath. But inflicting pain is the sociopath's avenue to pleasure, so that consideration would be way down on the list. This killer didn't have or take the time for torture.

I didn't want to run off in too many directions. Two bodies, no evidence, and no witnesses dictated the best idea was to keep an open mind.

"Eldon, do you think we might have a—"

The sound of the telephone ended our conversation.

Marty left to answer it while I picked up Mullen's file.

I pictured him and Lucy Jarvis on the docks, laughing and joking. Two faces in a boat load of faces. *Were Mullen and Lucy partners in a faulty scheme*? I didn't know.

What happened next was a crime I was very familiar with.

"Eldon, that was the clerk at Sheila's Mini Mart. A shoplifter just grabbed some stuff and took off."

"Was anyone hurt?"

"No, the clerk sounded more disgusted than scared. She says she knows the guy."

"Who is it?"

"She doesn't know his name, but he's done it before. I

called Charlie to give him the description, but he didn't answer. Should I call Reed?"

"No, I'll go. I need to get away from this desk."

Before Marty and I made it to the outer office, Charlie walked through the front door with a skinny, dark-haired kid in handcuffs. He placed the kid in the holding cell before approaching us with a huge smile on his face.

I knew this was going to be an interesting story.

"Talk about dumb luck. I was on my way to Sheila's to get a Coke when I see the kid there running across Gulf Boulevard. I pull into the parking lot, and this guy jumps out of his car and tells me the kid stole some food and stuff. I pull over to the beach access, 'cause that's where I saw him go, and there he sits, pretty as you please, eating pretzels and drinking a Red Bull."

"Good work, Charlie. Do we know his name?"

"Yeah, Winky Brisbane. Check his record, Marty. He's been caught shoplifting before."

"Winky Brisbane?" Marty said.

"They call him Winky 'cause he blinks all the time. Something about the sun bothering his eyes."

Marty and I glanced at the kid. It was true.

"And here's the rub, his folks have money. He doesn't have to steal, he just does it."

"I don't recall seeing anything on him before," Marty said.

"Nope, first time for us."

"How come you know so much about him?" I asked.

"Some of the guys at Billy's know him."

Billy's was a small bar in Indian Rocks Beach, and a favorite among local cops—a good place for them to unwind.

"Get him processed and take him to jail."

"You bet, Chief."

Charlie was smiling like he'd just nailed the FBI's Most Wanted.

"Now we know why Charlie didn't answer," Marty said, and crumpled the message.

I nodded and returned to my desk.

The Medical Examiner's report on Lucy Jarvis held my attention for about five minutes. I caught myself nodding off and admitted defeat. "I'm going home," I mumbled.

I looked at my watch. 3:47 p.m. When I looked up, I discovered Marty standing in the doorway again.

"Are you *finally* going home?"

"About time, don't you think?"

"Good! And make sure to get plenty of sleep."

"I will."

· · THREE · ·

I LIVE IN A SMALL HOUSE by the Intracoastal Waterway. My wife, Peg, and I fell in love with the place when we were house hunting. The neighborhood is quiet, mostly retirees, and I enjoy sitting on the patio after work. When Peg passed away three years ago, I considered putting the house up for sale, but couldn't bring myself to do it. The sunsets are magnificent. They remind me of the time I spent with her.

Half-way through my second beer, I heard someone knocking on the front door. I took another pull, got up, and went to find out the identity of my visitor.

"Marty! What happened? You get lost?"

"I thought you were going to get some sleep."

"I'm working on it."

"Doesn't look like it to me."

"Care to come in and have a beer?"

Her smile faded the minute she crossed the threshold.

"Eldon, I know you're tired, and I know talking about personal matters makes you uncomfortable, but could we talk?"

Over the years I'd become protective of Marty. A surrogate father if you will.

"I'll make an exception this time."

She sighed and lowered her eyes. "Am I weird?"

Ordinarily, I would have come up with a clever comeback, but not today.

"I don't think so. Is this about your boyfriend?"

"Yes…we're not going to see each other anymore."

"A mutual decision?"

"Zach says it's not working out. I thought we were doing great. We hadn't even had our first argument yet."

"Maybe that's what you wanted to believe."

"I never saw this coming. He never once mentioned that anything was wrong."

"Some guys are like that."

"And I seem to find all of them."

I took a swig of beer. "Marty, when it comes to romance, it's hard to tell what anyone will do."

"I must have done something to drive him away."

"You don't know that. Did you ask him the reason?"

"Yes, but he wouldn't tell me. Maybe he couldn't tell me, I don't know. He just said he was sorry and left." She looked up. "Eldon, do you suppose he left me because I work for the police?"

"Could be."

"But I told him where I worked when we first met."

"Maybe he thought he could handle it. Then he realized he couldn't."

"Then why did he keep asking me out?"

"Marty, people enter into relationships for different reasons. Maybe he wasn't looking for a permanent arrangement. And when it looked like you were getting serious, he—"

"Then why bother? Why put all your time and effort into someone if you're not looking for a permanent arrangement?"

I could tell she wasn't open to a varying opinion. "My advice to you, if you're asking for my advice, is to move on. One setback doesn't mean the end."

I saw a lone tear run down her cheek.

She wiped it away with the back of her hand. "Sorry. I didn't come here to cry on your shoulder."

"No problem, but if you're going to cry—"

"Actually, there's something I've been meaning to talk to you about it. More like *someone*, really."

"Are you being harassed?"

"No…well…lately I feel like I'm being followed." She shrugged. "Maybe I'm just being paranoid."

"What have you got to be paranoid about?"

"Nothing, that's just it, I can't imagine why anyone would be following me."

"Your boyfriend, maybe?"

"Even when I was with Zach. That's what's so weird."

"Did you notice anyone in particular in the places you went?"

"No one that stands out. Between what my father warned me about, and listening to you guys, I pay special attention to what's going on around me."

I looked down, searching hard for an answer. "Well, let's hope nothing comes of it." I raised my head and stared directly into her eyes. "But keep listening to your gut."

Marty offered a weak smile and nodded.

• • •

Marty had been gone an hour, and normally I'm in bed by nine or nine-thirty, but I'd lingered in my backyard because the evening was clear and cool. Having fallen asleep in what seemed like a matter of minutes, I was in the process of landing a big blue marlin. Battling the game fish sent an electrical charge through me, exhilarating. My adversary was close to giving up when a ringing sound drew my attention to the sky—then to the first mate—and finally out of my dream. I blinked twice and grabbed my cell phone.

"Sorry to wake you, Chief, but I've got a problem," Bo said.

I groaned. "What's wrong?"

"I…my keys are locked in the cruiser. I was patrolling the north end and thought I saw somebody behind Whiting's Hardware. I checked the rear of the building, and when I came back the cruiser was locked."

"Probably some kids. Call Barney and have him bring you the spare set from the office."

Silence preceded Bo's saying, "I'm sorry, Chief, but my radio's dead."

"Your hand-held radio?"

"I think it's the battery."

I released a sigh. "Do you have your cell phone?"

"Yeah, but I…can't remember his number."

"You remembered mine."

"I've got yours on my Contacts list."

I gave him Barney's number with hopes of returning to the Marlin. Of course, it didn't happen. Sometimes it's tough being the head man in a small town.

· · FOUR · ·

THE NEXT MORNING I WAS in my office reviewing the Mullen/Jarvis reports when I heard Marty enter. I was still tired and not in the best of moods.

Marty was glowing, upbeat, a complete reversal from the previous day.

"Good morning, Eldon."

"Morning, Marty. I need to issue a directive ASAP."

Her eyes widened. "Just a second." She scurried off to get a notepad and pen.

When she returned, I laid out the message simply and succinctly.

"Effective immediately—all car radios will be checked before the beginning of the shift and at the end of the shift. All hand-held radios will be checked before the beginning of the shift and placed in the chargers at the end of the shift. Furthermore, all employees will have the cell phone numbers of their co-workers in their possession during a shift." I paused a second. "That's it."

Marty finished writing and looked up. "Did something happen last night?"

"Nothing that can't be fixed."

"Okay, I'll get right on it."

I picked up the Forensics report on Lucy Jarvis.
Something about it, or the lack of something, sent my
curiosity into overdrive.

Forensics determined that a plastic gas container
was the cause of the fire, a container set in the middle
of the dock near the destroyed boats.

Somebody pissed somebody off, I thought.

Had the Jarvis woman seen the arsonist? Or had the
fire been set to lure her to her death? And why set the
container in the middle of the dock and not on a particular boat?

A gentle knocking made me look up from the report.

"I brought you some coffee," Marty said.

"Thanks. I can use it."

"Eldon, I want to thank you for last night. And I
apologize for dumping on you. I should be able to handle my own problems without involving you or anyone
else."

"No need to apologize. You know you can talk to me
any time."

"Good morning, Chief."

I looked around Marty and saw Reed Logan.

"Just the man I want to see."

I liked Reed. He reminded me of a fellow I knew at
the academy when I was starting out. I felt he was des-
tined for bigger and better things.

"Got a special assignment for me?"

"I want you to go to Whiting's Hardware first thing.
Bo thought he saw a prowler there last night."

Reed's eyes widened. "You think it might be the same guy who killed the woman and set the fire?"

Calm down, I thought. "I want you to have a look around and report back to me when you're done."

"Will do," he said.

Nodding to Marty, he left.

Marty's face became pensive. "Do you think it might have been our guy?"

"I don't know, but I'm not taking any chances. We know the time of night our suspect likes. This guy was spotted a little later."

"Our guy had already set the fires and killed Mullen and Jarvis by that time. It's possible he hadn't located his victim by then, I suppose, but his ability to escape without being seen suggests he's well prepared before he acts."

"What if he was scouting the area?" I asked. "Maybe he was in the process of piecing together his plan."

"It's possible, but I think he would do it during the day, you know, to blend in and seem less suspicious. Too many things can go wrong at night…like being seen."

"Well, let's hope it was just someone out for a late-night walk. Or a kid coming home from a date."

"We don't need any more excitement, that's for sure."

"Oh, call Bo and tell him to meet me at Whiting's."

Marty raised her eyebrows, nodded, and left. She knew.

It was possible Bo had inadvertently saved a life. And if he *had* seen our fire starter, I wanted a description—any description.

I picked up the telephone to call the Indian Rocks Beach Police Department. I looked at the receiver, thought twice about it, and hung up. Quite some time had passed since I'd seen Chief Roger Siddons. Like me, Roger was a cop who wanted to stay busy after putting in his time. I decided to pay my old friend a visit.

"Eldon Quick, how the hell are you?" Siddons said. "Have a seat. Did our boys in the fire department do a good job for you the other night?"

"I'm fine, Roger. And your boys did a great job."

"Good. Now what brings you all the way up here?"

I sat down and tried to get comfortable. "Did anything happen on the south end of town last night?"

"I'll talk to my guys when they come in. Why, did you have some trouble?"

"One of my men saw a prowler. I was just wondering if he'd been up your way."

Siddons offered a smile. "Eldon…normally you would call about something this petty. You got something brewing in your neck of the woods?"

"Nothing I can put a finger on. We've had two fires and two murders in two weeks. That's a lot of *two*s for my town."

"I'll say. I'll give you a call the minute I hear from my boys."

I'd just gotten into my SUV when I heard the radio crackle.

"Chief, its Bo, are you there?"

"Go ahead."

"Marty said you wanted to see me. I'm here at Whiting's."

"I'll be there in a minute."

I pictured Bo looking as bad as he sounded. He'd made a mistake, easy to forgive, but I could tell he was expecting the worst.

I pulled into Whiting's parking lot three minutes later.

Bo was parked on the north side of the building, leaning against his cruiser. As I approached him, he lowered his head.

"I'm sorry about last night, Chief."

"Forget it. Tell me what happened."

He snapped his head up and straightened. "I pulled in here last night to have a look around, just like always. That's when I saw somebody head around back. I parked the cruiser just about here and grabbed my flashlight. I guess he took off or was hiding 'cause I didn't see anybody. I looked around a little more, but nothing looked out of the ordinary. When I got back to the cruiser, it was locked. Chief, I'm really sorry."

"That's okay. Can you tell me anything about the person you saw?"

"Well...I *think* it was a man, but I didn't see his face. The lighting isn't good back there. But he wasn't tall. I know that for certain. No way he was six feet. And he wasn't heavy."

Bo stared at his shoes a moment. "But you know, Chief, he wasn't acting suspicious. I mean, most guys run right away if they're caught doing something. This guy just kept walking. He didn't act scared or anything."

"Did you find the keys?"

"They were on the seat. That's kind of strange, come to think of it. Why didn't he steal them?"

"To make us think it was kids. And to make sure you

couldn't come after him."

Rubbing the back of his neck, Bo looked down. "Yeah, I guess that's it."

"Keep an eye on Whiting's for a while, will you? Just in case he comes back."

"I sure will. Chief…Reed left right before you got here. He said you asked him to check things out."

"I did. Nothing against you, Bo, but I figured two pairs of eyes are better than one."

"Oh, well, he asked me why I was here, and I told him I was meeting with you. I told him about the prowler, too."

"That's okay, I already talked to him."

"Chief, I'd appreciate it not getting around that the keys were locked in my cruiser."

"Don't worry, that stays between you, me, and Barney."

Bo left in better spirits, left me feeling better, too. I got into my SUV and was about to leave when Marty came over the radio.

"I just talked to Reed. He said there was nothing out of the ordinary at Whiting's."

"Thanks, Marty."

"But he said he would look into it further."

I was glad to hear that. Another fire would bring more attention. The media had been kind to us so far, reporting only what we told them, not poking around. I wanted to keep it that way.

Calm fell over the department for the rest of the day. Not to say that it was quiet, but definitely not exciting.

Arriving at two conclusions, I did my best to view the crime scenes separately and simply. The fires and the murders were connected, or they weren't. Like I said, simple, but until I knew more, speculation would do nothing but cloud the issue.

About the time I decided I should revisit both crime scenes, Chief Roger Siddons called.

"Sorry I didn't get back to you sooner, Eldon. I got tied up with the council. You know how that goes."

"Unfortunately, I do. Nothing serious, I hope."

"Just the usual gabfest before the *Music Under the Moonlight* festival. Everybody wants to tell me how to do my job."

"I hear that."

"Anyway, my boys told me the south side of town was quiet last night. There were a few people making noise on the beach around eleven, but they were persuaded to tone it down."

"That's good to know."

"Anything new on your prowler?"

"We think it was a male, short of six feet in height. Not much to go on. Bo didn't get a good look at him."

"We'll keep an eye out just the same. We don't need a situation like...well, you know what I mean."

I knew exactly what he meant. I knew he was only trying to help.

"Eldon, what's the skinny on your murders? Do you have any leads?"

"Not a one. James Mullen was killed behind the Happy Clam. No evidence found. Lucy Jarvis was killed near the Oyster Point docks. Again, no evidence found." I paused. "They might be connected."

"Yeah, I heard that somebody nailed Mullet. He's been a guest at our place a time or two. I don't know the Jarvis woman."

"Might have been family related. You know fishermen."

Roger chuckled. "Keep me posted. I'll let you know if anything pops up here."

Sometimes talking things over can be a big help. Talking to Roger, I suddenly began to get the feeling that the Mullen/Jarvis murders *were* somehow connected. But for the time being I would look at them separately.

My mind started to wander to the thought of a cold beer on my patio. A soft knocking pulled me away as Marty walked into my office.

She appeared almost apologetic. "The honorable Sam Hackney is out front."

"I wonder whose dog got loose this time."

The words no sooner left my mouth when Sam barged past her.

"Excuse me, Marty. Just thought I'd check in to see how things are progressing, El."

I cringed inside at the sound of his voice. "Concerning what?"

"Come on, El, you know what I'm talking about. My phone's been ringing off the hook all day. The public wants some answers."

"Sam, when I have some answers, I'll let you know." I shot a quick glance at Marty.

"Oh, I thought you'd be close to making an arrest by now. Well, if there's anything I can do."

"I appreciate it, Sam."

His pseudo-sincerity made me sick. Politicians are only interested in one thing—votes. Sam was no different.

· · FIVE · ·

MY PATIO AND A COLD BEER were exactly what I needed. Seldom am I disappointed by this reward of quiet time. On this day the sunset obliged with a brilliant display. Pastel colors stretched out in both directions atop the fiery orb, joined by a narrow grouping of clouds, offering another unforgettable skyscape. Reflecting a burnt-orange underside, the clouds slowly drifted north, as if pointing the way to long, sought-after peace of mind.

A light supper accompanied by music from the *Alan Parsons Project* set the tone for an early trip to bed. Knowing that sleep can never be regained, I retired at 8:52 p.m., figuring I'd right my body until the next all-nighter.

I jumped awake at the sound of a siren screaming in the distance. Unfortunate, as I had been drifting through a state of unremembered dreams. Luminous hands on the nightstand clock glowed 11:23 p.m., disrupting my best laid plans. Waiting for the siren to fade,

I was surprised by its abrupt end. Seconds later, another pair of wailers broke the silence.

An urging too strong to ignore urged me to get dressed. There was no reason to go gallivanting through the night. Really, what could *I* do? Still, a gut feeling led me to my SUV and down Seafarer Lane to Gulf Boulevard. Turning north, pulsating red and blue lights came into view just inside the Indian Rocks Beach city line. Activity on the Gulf side was increasing due to an intense fire. Police cars barricaded the road as fire trucks roared to a halt.

Out of Deemer's Inlet, Gulf Boulevard remained two lanes before widening to four in the next block. This was a decided disadvantage to the fire department, exactly as it was with the Oyster Point docks fire.

I parked a block away and walked, stopping at the barricade with the rest of the curious onlookers. I searched the area for a familiar face, hoping Lieutenant O'Malley would be among the firefighters. I wanted to pick his brain after the commotion ended. Unable to find him, I wandered along the shoulder before stepping onto the sidewalk in front of a bait shop.

Flames raged above a storage building and lit up the faces of the men, women, and children around me. I scanned the crowd for the odd face—the one that displayed excitement as opposed to awe or sorrow. No one I saw expressed such emotion. A moment later, it hit me.

The subject of my obsession had no interest in the fire. If my hunch was correct, the killer would mingle with the crowd, waiting and pretending to be captivated before stealing away for the kill. A target selected, he would be subtle, calculated, until the perfect time and place presented itself.

I stepped to the edge of the building for a better field of vision, slowly pivoting my head from side to side. Locating an object is easier using this method, a fact unknown by most. I hoped what I'd learned from fighter pilots would help locate a killer—if he was there.

On my third pass, a voice inside my head told me to stop and look over my shoulder.

Lit only by a single streetlamp, the area toward the rear of the bait shop appeared less than inviting.

I walked to the back of the undersized building and discovered an asphalt pad of equal width. Spreading to the seawall along the Intracoastal Waterway, it was wide enough for a sanitation truck to empty the dumpster by the rear exit. The area contained nothing of interest to anyone passing by. However, I spotted something on the southeast corner of the pad. After glancing behind me, I began a deliberate hike in the direction of the object.

My curiosity was satisfied when I determined a body was lying by the seawall. In the poor lighting, I knelt down and placed two fingers on the man's neck but felt no pulse.

His light-colored jacket looked clean and absent of dirt or blood. His blue jeans and running shoes looked brand new, not typical of those working the fishing boats. I figured him to be a local or a visitor, not that it mattered. He was dead. And *that* was all that mattered.

I carefully retraced my steps and went back to the barricade, approaching a sergeant I'd seen when I arrived.

He seemed less than impressed when I produced my badge.

"Sergeant, I need you to come with me," I said.

He looked at the fire then back at me. "Chief, with all due respect, I'm kinda busy right now."

"It's important...and bring your flashlight."

He did as I requested and walked with me to the rear of the bait shop. Arriving at the edge of the seawall, his attitude quickly changed.

"Ho-lee cow! This is turning into one hell of a night!"

The beam from his flashlight made for an interesting discovery. The victim's jacket turned out to be a pale green—irrelevant—but traces of bruising were beginning to appear on his neck.

"Better cordon off this area and alert your crime scene people, Sergeant."

"Yes, sir, I'll get right to it." He started to leave but stopped and tilted his head around. "Chief, call me curious, but why were you walkin' around back here? Did you see someone?"

I took a few steps toward him. "Sergeant, you've no doubt heard about what's going on in my town?"

"Sure, two fires and two murders. Who hasn't heard about...oh, wait! You came back here because you thought..."

"Right, so for now let's keep it between you and me and the sea. I'll contact Chief Siddons tomorrow."

An unhappy expression shaped his face as he turned to leave. He knew. Three murders made for more than coincidence. By law, it was the factor for the definition of a serial killer.

· · SIX · ·

IN THE NEXT TWO WEEKS we heard no more from the supposed serial killer. The fact that no other murders occurred lent credence to the assumption the killer had moved on. I'm not prone to relaxing simply because of a lull in activity. True, we had no suspects, never did, but I wasn't about to admit defeat. I followed a few leads from less-than-desirable sources, but they turned out to be personal issues—finger-pointing—and the alibis solid enough to dismiss the accused.

I made a mental note to pick a day and question the fishermen at the Oyster Point docks. I didn't expect much cooperation because boat people are a tight-lipped group when it comes to dealing with the law. It would probably turn out to be a waste of time, but it had to be done.

My critics were silenced by time and everyday responsibilities keeping them occupied, but the topic was brought up again and again at town meetings and by social groups. Sam Hackney was the biggest boil on my butt, no surprise since he was up for re-election the coming year. When he summoned me to his office to discuss Deemer Days and Nights, the town's annual seafood festival, I knew the subject would be on the table at some point.

"Glad you could spare the time, El. Have a seat."

"It's never a problem, Sam."

The mayor's office is a small room inside the small town hall building, made smaller by a desk befitting the man's ego. I sat down knowing we were about to discuss what we discussed ever year. I hoped that was *all* we discussed.

"The council and I have been tossing around some ideas about the seafood festival. We want this year to be the best ever."

You say that every year, I thought.

"It's shaping up nicely. We have more restaurants involved, a local band for entertainment, and something new—a cigar and wine tent. That was my idea."

"Sounds like it should be a huge success."

"We do have one area of concern, and I want your input."

Here it comes.

"We're concerned about security. Do you think we should hire some extra people as a precaution?"

In the past, concerns ranged from the limited parking issue to adding a stupid attraction called Dunk the Police Chief.

"I don't think it's necessary, Sam. Our problems are relatively minor. We're always going to have some folks who get carried away."

"I understand, but in light of what happened

recently, I would hate to have anything spoil our wonderful celebration."

"Are you talking about the murders, Sam?"

He said nothing and let his eyes speak for him.

I folded my arms. "Nothing has happened in weeks. Why would you assume the worst?"

He leaned forward, placed both elbows on his desk, and rested his chin on his clasped hands. "You haven't caught him, have you? To my knowledge, Indian Rocks Beach hasn't caught him, either. That means he's still out there. And if he's still out there, he could strike again."

"Why would you think he'd be gutsy enough to try something in a crowd of people, especially during a festival? He sets fires at night and goes after isolated targets."

"Exactly my point. With extra security guards he'd be less likely to try anything."

"I'll assign an additional patrolman to watch the festival grounds."

"Overtime? I'm not certain the council will approve the added expense."

"You want to hire private security guards. What's the difference?"

"The money to pay the security company will come from the festival budget, and not the city budget."

"Sam, I don't believe we'll need an army. If money is that big a concern, then *I'll* put in the overtime. I'm on salary. You won't have to touch either budget."

"You feel certain we'll be safe."

Great, he wants guarantees. "Sam, I can't be certain of anything. His pattern of behavior suggests he's moving to the north of us."

Sam leaned back in his chair. "Pattern of behavior, huh? What does Indian Rocks say?"

"About what?"

"About his pattern of behavior, El. What do they think?"

I sighed. "Right now, fire is the common denominator. There's nothing to indicate that it's even the same perpetrator."

Silence filled the void between us.

"Maybe I should call a special council meeting and put the security issue to a vote," Sam offered.

I stared hard at him resisting the urge to tell him what he could do with his suggestion.

"Okay, El. I'll abide by your decision. I hope you understand and appreciate the council's concern."

I nodded.

Every year, I do.

The short walk down the hall allowed me time to release anxiety. I despised these yearly meetings before the seafood festival. I suppose Sam felt it his duty to keep the lines of communication open, but it was getting old.

No area large enough existed on the Gulf side, so we used the same park every year. Being across the street from Town Hall, the park provided easy access to the volunteers setting up the barricades. We employed the same company for the tents, and the majority of their workers could raise them in their sleep. Placement of the vendors seldom varied, so few problems arose when they arrived. A scant number of small rides were brought in by the same company for the younger children. This was our festival, and not counting the different themes for the kids' costume contest, repetition was the mainstay.

I entered the office and was greeted by a smiling Marty.

"Pow-wow done so soon? I figured you'd be gone another hour."

"Sam has laryngitis."

"Really?"

"No."

She laughed. "I posted a schedule for the guys with the usual overlapping of shifts and minimum overtime."

"I'm sure the council will be pleased with your diligence."

"Oh, are they on your back again?"

"Always. This year they're concerned about security."

"Because of what...but it's been quiet for some time now."

"The council is worried because we haven't caught him yet. I told Sam he'd just have to wait because Spiderman was still on vacation."

"Eldon, you didn't."

"I didn't."

"I ran a search of the Tampa Bay area. No other community has had any similar criminal activity."

"Good, maybe our boy got caught."

"I don't think so. I didn't find any arrests for arson, and the murders were either domestic or associated with robberies."

"I hope to hell he hasn't moved on. Maybe we got lucky and somebody killed him."

Marty bit her bottom lip. "There *was* one thing, though. Clearwater P.D. responded to a disturbance call last Tuesday morning at 3:11 a.m. An argument followed by gunshots."

"That doesn't sound like our boy."

"The address is a Clearwater Beach motel that's for sale. Shortly afterward, a woman was found shot to death a block away on the beach."

Although a different *modus operandi*, another diversion resulted in the discovery of a body. I could see the red flags fluttering and remembered Barney's assessment: "Maybe no, maybe so."

"I wanted to check with you before digging any deeper."

"Hold off on doing that. I don't want to get another agency involved until we're certain."

"I sure hope Sam doesn't find out."

"I'll fish that stream when I come to it. And Marty, for now this stays between you and me and the sea. I don't need the council getting all worked up because they're ignorant of police work."

"Yes, sir," she said, and saluted.

"Will you stop doing that!"

An impish gleam appeared in her eyes. Then she rocked her head from side to side.

"Okay, what's going on?"

"What?"

"You. I've seen you in a good mood before, but today you seem in an *exceptionally* good mood. What gives?"

She looked around to make sure we were alone. "I met a guy."

"Good for you. He's not like that other guy, is he?"

"No, he's not at all like Zach. He's clever and funny and *really* good looking."

"Where'd you meet him?"

"At Ripples. Janie, Claire, and I went dancing last Saturday night."

"Oh, boy."

Janie and Claire were Marty's best friends and a fun-loving duo—but a little on the wild side.

"Do you want to hear about Seth or not?"

"I do, but not right now."

"I think you'll like him."

"We'll see."

"I'd like you to meet him, you know, when you have the time." She looked down and began playing with some papers on her desk.

I sighed. "Okay. When?"

"Well...since you *always* make an appearance at the festival...and if you just *happened* to be there between two and three on Saturday...we might *accidently* run into you."

"I'll see what I can do."

"Good!"

"You're a little conniver, you know that?"

Marty's face glowed. "I kno-o-o-w."

I went to my office and took a seat.

I quickly forgot about Marty's new friend. I couldn't dismiss the notion that the dead woman found on Clearwater Beach would wind up on the list of our killer's victims. No notice of state-wide or national alerts regarding a specific serial killer had crossed my desk—Marty was good about keeping me informed—and the modus operandi of other high-profile cases didn't fit the fellow we were after.

I've always been a worrier of sorts. My wife used to say it's what made me a good cop. Over the years I'd managed to rid myself of the sleepless nights and the acid-stomach episodes, but every once in a while, a case would latch onto me and not let go.

Retirement calmed my nerves and improved my

health. I figured this job would amount to nothing more than being a glorified dog catcher. I remember thinking, *how difficult can it be*? Feuding neighbors, a few fender benders, inebriated tourists—a slam dunk compared to Miami. Until now, I'd been right.

I leaned back and debated making an official call to the Clearwater Police Department. Setting off a false alarm by implying the existence of a serial killer wouldn't be practical. I could hear them now. "Little Deemer's Inlet is all a-twitter!" "Oh, lordy, what're they gonna do?" By the same token, sitting on my hands and being found out later would win me no favor in the law enforcement community. I was about to pick up the phone when Marty knocked on the door.

"Sam wants to talk to you."

I shook my head. "I don't believe that guy."

Marty turned on her heels and disappeared.

Mumbling a few choice obscenities, I picked up the telephone.

"El, we've got a problem!"

"What is it, Sam?"

"The kiddie rides company just called. They're bowing out of the festival."

"Correct me if I'm wrong, but shouldn't you be talking to Sten? This kind of thing falls under the town manager's job description."

"Sten Knutson doesn't know a kiddie ride from shineola. I don't know why we hired him."

Because he came cheap, I thought.

"El, you know a lot of people. Can you help me?"

Fact was I didn't know that many people. I sighed. "Okay, I'll see what I can do."

"I knew I could count on you. Stop by the cigar tent

this weekend. Cigars are on me."

I paused after I hung up the phone. "Marty, would you step in here, please."

Tentative best described her expression when she entered my office.

"Were you listening in on my conversation with Sam?"

"Eldon, I would *never* do such a thing."

"I thought I heard you laughing."

"It wasn't me…I…he told me what was wrong when he called."

"I want you to take charge of finding another company for the festival."

Her mouth dropped open. "Why me?'

"It's called delegating responsibility."

·· SEVEN ··

MUCH TO THE RELIEF OF SAM and the council, Marty was able to find another kiddie rides company willing to help us. Although fewer rides came at a higher cost, averting disaster made me a hero for a day. I sent a text to Spiderman letting him know he wouldn't have to cut short his stay in Cabo San Lucas.

Even though the unsolved murders still loomed over the community, the festival became the main focus, my department included. We expected the minor incidents, misdemeanors, and mischief, mainly, and I knew my staff would handle them in a thorough and efficient manner.

The opening ceremonies commenced with Sam Hackney spouting his usual balloon juice before the fun began. Swarms of people arrived, surprising but welcomed, and the aroma of boiled shrimp, smoked mullet, fried crab cakes and other seafood delights hung heavy in the air.

All was quiet in the hours after the festival shut down,

and right up until it all started again the next day.

On Saturday, I strolled into the park a little after one p.m. greeted by handshakes and back slaps. Celebrity in a small town is ingratiating, and at the same time, annoying. Taken for granted on a daily basis, I suddenly became the object of praise and numerous questions.

"You're doing a fine job, Eldon. Any progress with the murders?"

"Glad you're here to protect us, Chief. We feel safer knowing you're around."

"Does this maniac start a fire every time he kills someone?"

"Did you ever consider that the killer might be someone who lives here?"

Every year I was showered with adulation, and every year I accepted it humbly. This year was different. This year a killer took center stage, and I was reduced to the role of assuring folks that we would catch him.

In the middle of munching fried grouper nuggets and corn fritters, I spied Marty with her new friend. Watching them interact proved to be an interesting behavioral study. The movements, the body language, the cutting of glances on both their parts became a ceremonial dance. He would point to a certain delicacy. She would make a face and shake her head. He'd shrug, she'd laugh—all the signs of subtle seduction.

When they drew near me, Marty did a double-take then shifted her eyes back to her friend. Closer still, I continued to eat, acting the oblivious co-star in her movie. I made certain my mouth was empty when they got within speaking range.

"Why Eldon, what're you doing here?" Marty said.

"I couldn't resist sampling this delicious seafood."

I set my eyes on her friend and smiled.

"Seth Russell, this is Chief Eldon Quick."

I wiped the grease from my fingers and extended my hand. "Pleasure to meet you, Seth."

"Likewise, Chief. I'm surprised you're not in uniform today."

"They're all at the cleaners."

His staccato laughter reminded me of a cartoon character—an annoying cartoon character.

"Seth and I are trying to decide what to eat," Marty said.

"Is she always this finicky, Chief?"

"Since the day I met her. Why, I remember one time—"

"All right, that's enough," Marty interrupted. "Just because I'm careful about what I eat is no reason to make fun of me."

Seth and I exchanged looks.

"Of course it is," we said in unison.

Marty rolled her eyes. "I can see nothing but trouble ahead."

Seth's cartoon laughter sounded again. "Looks like quite a crowd today. Are there always this many people?"

"Depending upon tomorrow, we may be looking at a record," I said.

"Do you have the manpower in the event some idiot does something stupid?"

"We're prepared for any situation."

His question didn't bother me as much as the tone of his voice. Inquiring is much different than interrogating. His scanning of the crowd reminded me of a tiger on the hunt—a trait accentuated by his close-set brown eyes.

"So, what do you do for a living?" I asked.

"I'm in sales, automotive and industrial batteries. I just moved here two months ago."

"You live in Deemer's Inlet?"

"No, I live in St Petersburg." He laughed. "Over by the Handy Bridge. Most of my prospects are in Tampa."

"He means the Gandy Bridge," Marty said. "He calls it the Handy Bridge because it's convenient for his ride to Tampa."

"Where do you hail from?" I asked.

"Illinois, the Chicago area. My company had an opening down here, and I was tired of the cold winters anyway. It worked out perfectly."

Another one, I thought. "How do you like it so far?"

"It's great! This is my first time in Florida. I had no idea the weather could be so wonderful."

Check with me again in July.

"Well, Eldon, I know Seth is hungry, so I'd better get him something to eat," Marty said.

"She's right, Chief, but when you can spare some time, I'd like to talk fishing with you."

"Name the place and I'll be there."

I watched them continue past the vendors, and chuckled when they elected to go with conch salad and bottled water. I had a feeling that Seth would have preferred smoked mullet and a beer.

I continued to eat my food, happy to see Marty in good spirits again. She wasn't the sort to go through life alone. I wasn't, either. I'd simply learned to accept it.

The day moved on with more folks mingling and eating until the festival shut down at ten o'clock right on schedule—without occurrence.

Deciding to remain and oversee the clean-up instead of heading home and returning at midnight, I strolled across the street and leaned against my SUV.

A cruiser pulled up in front of Town Hall, and Barney Andrews joined me.

"How'd it go, Chief?"

"Without a hitch, I'm glad to say."

"All quiet in the woods, too. Marty got her a new boyfriend?"

"Who told you?"

Barney smiled—as if I should know.

"Yeah, he seems like a nice guy. I talked to them this afternoon."

"What's he do?"

"Sells batteries for some company out of Chicago."

"Batteries, huh? I need a new battery for muh boat. Maybe I'll give 'im a call."

Now I was smiling. If anyone could get information out of Seth Russell, Barney was the man. His easy-going style could charm the CIA.

"Know much 'bout him?"

"Only that he's new to the area."

Barney nodded. "You gonna check 'im out?"

"First thing Monday morning."

"Well, I gotta answer the call o' nature and then the call o' duty. See ya around, Chief." He turned to leave but stopped. "Any chance we can get some fishin' in soon?"

"I'll let you know, Barney. Sam Hackney's on my butt again about those murders."

"If ya ask me, I think that feller's done moved on… and speakin' of movin' on."

I watched him enter Town Hall wanting to believe he was right.

The clean-up was winding down, and the park would soon be dark.

I was about to climb into my SUV when a familiar sound split the evening air. In the distance, sirens screamed and sent adrenaline coursing through my body.

Is it him? Only one way to find out.

I roared out of the parking lot and sped south toward Hidden Rocks Beach. I wouldn't wait this time. I'd locate the highest-ranking officer, have him place a call for back-up then begin a search of the perimeter. With luck, we'd nail the bastard before he got away.

In the scant amount of time it took me to get to the scene, reason took over and the spike of adrenaline fueling me leveled out. I rethought my approach.

I had no basis, let alone the authority to go charging in and barking orders. And ranting like a lunatic certainly wouldn't help. I couldn't stand around like I'd done before, either. A fine line between reticence and overreaction had to be walked, and I knew how to do it.

I pulled into the parking lot of a convenience store and left my SUV, moving at a quick but even pace toward the activity.

One of the first things I noticed was an absence of fire/rescue trucks, which made sense as I got closer. There *was* no fire. Instead, three deputies formed a wall in front of a small group of people. Two more stood guard over a couple of men. My initial thought was a fight that had ended with the arrival of the Sheriff's Office.

My energy level dropped, a good feeling actually,

and I quietly chided my over-active imagination. My plan to escape before being recognized was thwarted when a voice sounded behind me.

"Looking for some excitement, Chief?"

I turned around and eyed my accuser. "You got me, Sergeant. I have a secret passion for bar fights."

We both laughed and shook hands.

Deputy Sergeant Mark Roush and I had met the previous year at a conference in Orlando.

"Well, you've come to the right place. Hannigan's gets lively two or three times a month. How's it going up your way?"

"We've got the seafood festival this weekend. Outside of that, it's been pretty quiet."

Roush said nothing, smiling and waiting.

I didn't know him that well but knew his reputation. On the job, he viewed everything with a serious eye.

"Mark, I guess you heard about the murders."

"Yeah, two in two weeks, wasn't it?"

I told him about the fires, my discovery in Indian Rocks Beach, and the lack of evidence and suspects.

"So naturally, when you heard the sirens you thought your perp might be at it again."

"Right now I'm feeling very foolish."

"Tell you what, after we haul these guys to jail, I'll have my men take a look around."

A short time later the combatants were taken away, the crowd dispersed, and the remaining deputies fanned out around the bar.

Roush and I crossed Gulf Boulevard and began to check the open areas and between the buildings. We agreed to head south a few blocks then swing back along the beach.

"What's your take on this guy, Chief?"

"For one thing, he's bold. He sets fires at times when he could easily get caught. I believe he selects his targets in advance then somehow manages to get them alone. I don't know why his victims are chosen. The first was a man, the second, a woman. The only connection being they worked the fishing boats. The third, in Indian Rocks Beach, was an accountant, young fellow, and I have no idea what his connection to the others might be. *If* there's a connection at all."

Roush pursed his lips. "All told you're dealing with arson, murder, and victims differing in gender and appearance. That's going to be tough to profile."

An access sign decorated with seashells and starfish presented a path for us to begin our search of the beach. Almost immediately, we discovered the presence of others.

A considerable number of night walkers lined the shore, not unusual for the start of a weekend. The sky was clear and the weather perfect for those desiring a moonlit stroll.

Roush and I headed north struggling through sugar sand, with the moon providing enough light to help us avoid any obstacles. An unproductive search resulted in our decision to return to Gulf Boulevard.

"I want to thank you for your time and help, Mark."

"My pleasure, Chief. Actually, I'm glad we *didn't* find a body."

For some reason I glanced to my left and peered across the street.

A man outside of Hannigan's caught my eye. It was Seth Russell. Alone.

I watched him get into his car and leave the parking

lot, driving right past us, unaware of our being there.

Two of the three deputies waited on the sidewalk in front of Hannigan's. After we reached them, they told us they'd found nothing.

"Torrelli is still out," the shortest said.

"Stay in touch, Chief. Maybe we can find time for a little fishing."

I nodded and was about to leave when I heard his radio crackle.

"Sergeant, I'm five blocks south in the alley behind the dry cleaners. You need to see this."

"That's Torrelli," Roush said to me. "Care to ride along?"

Accompanying Roush in his cruiser, I flashed back to my first meeting with Seth Russell and his annoying laughter.

· · EIGHT · ·

MUCH TO MY DISMAY, but not to my surprise, we found another body.

A woman no more than thirty years old sat propped up against a small picket fence enclosing two garbage cans. Her head was tilted downward with her chin on her chest, and blood saturated the ends of her long flaxen hair. A swath of crimson painted the front of her pink blouse, evidence that she, like Lucy Jarvis, died from an opening of the throat.

"She's still warm, Sergeant. It must have just happened," Torrelli said.

The three of us looked at one another.

"He might still be in the neighborhood," Roush said. He glanced over his shoulder. "Torrelli, tell Eamons and Toojay to check all the streets around Hannigan's. Five blocks in each direction. You and Strong go back to the bar and nose around."

The vision of Seth Russell grew stronger as I watched Torrelli hustle away.

"I guess I'd better call Homicide and Forensics," Roush added.

I nodded and looked down at the asphalt alley. *So much for footprints or tire tracks*, I thought.

Roush placed the calls and joined me by the woman's body.

Her arms were stretched across the top of the fence, and wrists locked between the slats.

"What do you make of the way she's positioned, Chief?"

"Like a crucifixion."

"Think it might be intentional? A message or something?"

"I couldn't say, but I know one thing. If it's the guy I'm looking for then he's getting bolder. And that's not good."

Roush shook his head. "But Chief, how could your guy know there would be a fight? And how could he know that she would be here? We're five blocks away from Hannigan's."

"Maybe they were on a date. Maybe he convinced her to leave when the fight broke out."

"So...we're looking at a guy who acts when the opportunity arises? No set plan or compulsion?" Roush stepped back and began to windmill the area with his eyes. "The only blood I see is on her. You'd think there'd be some on the ground."

I imitated him. "Maybe he killed her in his car?"

"But Chief—"

"I know. There should be a blood trail...or at least some spattering when he dumped her."

As I pondered the inexplicable, my mind went into overdrive. There are more serial killers throughout the country than the public wants to believe. Sociopaths, psychopaths, all of them manage their evil undetected. Sooner or later, though, even the wiliest among them slip up. I wanted this one caught sooner rather than later.

"Mark, would you ask your detective to call me when he's done here?"

"Sure thing, Chief."

On my way home I decided not to wait until Monday to investigate Seth Russell. My unexpected sighting of him at Hannigan's bothered me. The man could do what he wanted on his own time—his right. His designs on Marty placed him under the umbrella of personal involvement—my business, in other words. No way was she going to be the next victim. Not if I could help it.

Eeriness hung over the darkened outer office as I passed through, strange because the décor hadn't changed in seven years. Marty's desk sat in its usual location yet seemed unfamiliar and out of place. The filing cabinets against the far wall now appeared threatening, as if waiting to rise up and bury me under a mountainous gray pile. Even the fronds of the foxtail palms brushing the windows outside sounded different, odd because I'd spent many nights alone with paperwork, never giving a thought to the void beyond my office door. Tonight, though, a stranger lurked—my imagination—creeping between the rows of logic and reason, intent upon defiling my sanity.

After turning on the office light, I sat down at my desk and forced my computer to cooperate. If the data on Russell provided even an inkling of suspicion, we'd bring him in for questioning. Diplomacy, be damned! I could handle apologizing to Marty, but no way was I going to sit by and watch her walk toward certain death.

The information filing across my computer screen told an interesting tale of the battery salesman. He hadn't lied about being from Chicago. Not divulging the route he'd taken to get there became a telling list of states and companies.

Besides Illinois, his landing points in the recent past were Michigan, Wisconsin, Iowa, Oklahoma, and Arkansas. He'd promoted a variety of products, and his stay in each locale never exceeded two years. Either he'd opted for a better situation, or he was a lousy salesman. No criminal record appeared in any of those states, not even a parking ticket—a discovery that eased my mind to a degree.

I remembered that Marty's search turned up no similar crimes in the area, and I began to feel better about their relationship. Better, but not convinced. Maybe my reluctance to welcome Seth with open arms was due to my first impression of him. I realized that to be successful in sales one must be outgoing and personable, but the trick is to sound sincere. While Seth seemed friendly enough, he came across as guarded, as if he invited only those he trusted into his world. I wondered who, if anyone, he trusted. And I had a feeling that he possessed the ability to read people easily. How he chose to utilize that ability as far as his relationship with Marty was cause for concern—a concern for me, anyway. I'd gladly accepted the responsibility of making certain, by whatever means possible, that her vulnerability remained unexploited. Keeping my nose out of her personal life was an exercise that dogged me every day.

I could tell by the way Marty spoke of Seth that she was willing to open every door to him. Maybe it was the nature of my profession that brought about suspicion. Maybe it was my nature in general.

Thinking back, I remembered the manner in which he paid attention to the crowd at the festival. Like the eyes of a hunter in search of his target, a predator knowing exactly the right moment to descend upon his prey.

An unexpected chill sent a shiver through me as the memory of Marty's uneasiness about being watched entered my mind. Was Seth the shadow matching her every move? His time in the area would be enough to select a mark and study their habits and routines, his good looks and personality the undeniable magnet of attraction. Could it be that *he* was the serial killer roaming our streets?

Four victims discovered in the aftermath of as many incidents was a fact I couldn't ignore. Witnessing Seth's presence prior to one of those discoveries kept me from dismissing him as a person of interest. My solution was simple. Meet with him one-on-one, and get him to talk more about his background.

Finally, fatigue pulled me from my desk and ordered me home. At the outer office door, I stopped and glanced over my shoulder.

• • NINE • •

WHEN I FINALLY ROUSED THE FOLLOWING DAY, I felt as though I hadn't slept at all. The alarm clock welcomed me with a wonderful sight: 3:37 p.m.

Good, too late to go to the festival, I thought. I was about to roll over when my cell phone rang. *Lord, what have I done to deserve this?*

"Chief, it's Logan."

"What's up?" I mumbled.

"I was hoping to catch you at the festival."

"Nah, I had a late night. Is anything wrong?"

"No, I just forgot to tell you that I have a dentist appointment tomorrow morning."

"Not a problem, *I'll* cover for you if I have to."

"Thanks, Chief. It shouldn't take too long. I keep the choppers in good shape."

"Good for you. See you tomorrow." I rolled over, thinking, *Now where was I?*

My phone rang again.

"Eldon, how come you're not at the festival?"

"I had a late night, Marty. You're at the festival again?"

"Seth wanted to come back. I've never seen anyone eat so much."

"Conch salad isn't very filling."

"*Ha-ha*, very funny."

"What's on your mind?"

"Eldon, I'd like to invite you over for dinner one night this week. Seth doesn't know many people, and I'd like you two to get acquainted. You don't mind, do you?"

You're moving awfully fast, girl. "Let's discuss it tomorrow."

"Uh, sure, okay. Are you all right? You don't sound well."

"I'm just tired."

"Uh-oh, I'd better make the coffee extra strong tomorrow."

I closed my eyes and began to drift again. In no time I was sitting in a boat on the Gulf of Mexico, miles away from shore. I cast a line into the blue-green water and settled back. Beneath an azure sky adorned with horse-tail clouds, I listened to the waves lapping the hull and felt the wisp of a breeze from the west. The fishing rod began to twitch and jump, and the line released a high-pitched buzz as it left the reel.

When my phone rang a third time, I almost threw it across the room.

"El, you missed the closing ceremonies!"

"Sorry, Sam, I overslept."

"Overslept? But it's...oh, well, never mind. Say, El, what's this I hear about a murder in Hidden Rocks Beach? People have been asking me about it all day."

Probably the local gossip committee, I thought. I wasn't about to pour fuel on the fire by giving him any information. "I've been asleep, Sam."

"A woman's body was found near Hannigan's Bar. Do you think it was—?"

"You know a rough crowd hangs out at Hannigan's, Sam. I wouldn't worry about it."

"I suppose you're right. I was just thinking…anyway, the ceremony was magnificent. My speech had the park ringing with applause."

"Congratulations. How's it looking over there?"

"Orderly, efficient, the clean-up's in full swing. I think we set a record for attendance this year."

"That's good to hear."

"Say, El, the council wants to meet with you this week. Evaluation time, you know. Let's figure out a day to make that happen."

"I'll call you tomorrow, Sam."

I rolled over and closed my eyes.

If that phone rings again, I'm getting my gun.

• • TEN • •

MONDAY MORNING BEGAN EARLY, five a.m. according to the clock in my office. Having never left my bed on Sunday, I'd managed a few hours of rest after the interruptions. I was ready for the day, and felt good, in fact. Unlike my previous visit, the old office embraced my presence, withdrew its shadowy countenance, and gave me the confidence to face the challenge of leadership.

I leveled my eyes on the Mullen/Jarvis files with nagging uncertainty. I was missing something. I was positive that a connection between the two existed and bringing it to light was my mission.

I retrieved a legal-sized pad from my desk drawer and drew several equally spaced lines top to bottom. I titled each column with the names of the victims and began noting bits of information. Nit-picking became the first order.

Mullen: *found in dunes-eyes open-beginning rig-or-wallet on person.*

Jarvis: *found by docks-eyes closed-no rigor-identity*

(at time) unknown.

The similarities came next: *same profession-found after or during fire-distance from fire marginal-no signs of struggle.*

I could have gone into greater detail, but this would do for a start.

Flipping the page, I created two more columns labeled *Indian Rocks Beach* and *Hidden Rocks Beach.* After noting all I could remember, I removed the top sheet, placed it beside the pad, and began to study the facts.

I'd learned from Chief Roger Siddons that the victim found behind the bait shop was an accountant named Raymon Jbara. His firm, located in Clearwater, brought to mind the woman found on Clearwater Beach. I purposely omitted a column on her because I had no available information because of my reluctance to involve the Clearwater Police Department.

Jbara, age twenty-three, recently moved to Indian Rocks Beach from Tampa. I assumed him to be a novice accountant. Too bad his first job wound up being his last.

The thought of contacting the FBI wandered into my mind as I continued to study the facts. They had specialists to deal with serial killers, and resources far greater than any we possessed. But bringing them in would cause a stir within the community, and that was the last thing I wanted. Something needed to be done, though, and soon. Fully engrossed in the gathered facts before me, I lost track of the time.

"Here's your coffee, Eldon," Marty said.

I looked up, surprised I hadn't heard her. "Thanks, Marty. You didn't make it extra strong, did you?"

Marty smiled as the she placed the cup in front of me. "No, a man your age should be cutting back on caffeine anyway."

"So I've heard."

She glanced at my desk and leaned forward. "What's this?"

"What?"

"This," she said, and tapped the pad. "Since when do you care about what goes on in Hidden Rocks Beach?"

"Oh, this? Just some notes I made on…"

"I heard about the woman on the news this morning."

I leaned back in my chair. "Okay, you got me."

"You think he struck again, don't you?"

Marty was *too* good.

"I do."

"How did you hear about it?"

"You're not the only one who watches the news."

Marty cocked her head and stared with probing eyes.

I sighed. "Saturday night. After the festival. I heard sirens and…"

"You couldn't help yourself. You just *had* to go down there."

"Turned out to be a fight at Hannigan's. I recognized one of the deputies and asked him to look around."

"*You* found her?"

"No, one of the deputies."

"Was it the same as before?"

"In some regards."

I gave her the details, but left out the part about seeing Seth.

"Are you going to call Clearwater P.D.?"

"Probably. I'm waiting to hear from the sheriff's office first."

Marty looked down, thinking. "What are you going to tell Sam? He's bound to find out one way or the other."

"He already knows about the murder, but nothing else. Do me a favor. From now on when he calls, take a message."

"Eldon, that's only going to make him mad."

"Too bad. I don't need him or any of the council sticking their noses into this."

"Okay." She shook her head.

Reed Logan started into my office, saw us then stepped back. I waved him in.

"Reporting for duty, Chief."

Marty laughed as she turned to leave.

"That was fast."

"Just a check-up, I have an understanding with my dentist."

"I guess so. Well, there's been no excitement so far."

Reed walked to the side of my desk. He looked over his shoulder before addressing me.

"So, tell me about the fight at Hannigan's."

I held my surprise in check. "Don't you listen to the news?"

He folded his arms and grinned. "I saw you standing out front when I drove by. How many people went to jail?"

"Two. The crowd made it look worse."

"Boy, that place is a hotbed of trouble. I'm glad we don't have anything like that around here."

Something about his demeanor raised a question. "Another hot date Saturday night?"

"And how! What a girl! We started with dinner at *Rollo's*, and then we went dancing at the *Surfin' Bird* in St. Pete Beach."

"Anyone special?"

"Nancy? Not really. We've dated a few times. She surprised me, though, when she invited me to her place for drinks."

"Where does she live?"

"Indian Shores. She's got a condo right on the beach. That's where we were going when I saw you. And, boy, did she make me feel right at home. We sat on the balcony a while looking at the Gulf, then she suggested we—"

"Excuse me," Marty said, and stuck her head through the doorway. "There's been an accident at Seaside Avenue and Gulf Boulevard."

"I'll tell you about it later, Chief."

When I heard the door to the outer office close, I focused on Marty.

"What do you think of Reed?"

Marty gave me a puzzled look. "I think he's an okay guy. He's a little overzealous at times, but that's to be expected. I don't have a problem with him."

"Did he ever ask you out?"

The lines on her face grew deeper.

"Yes, but I told him I don't date co-workers. He never asked me again."

"Has he ever bothered you?"

"No. Is there something about him I should know?"

"Not really."

"Then why are you asking me these questions?"

"Because, I don't want any problems arising between the members of my crew."

"There's *never* been a problem between any of your men and me."

"Good, that's all I wanted to know."

"Right, and three nights a week I moonlight as a stripper."

Thankfully, the telephone interrupted us before she could back me into a corner.

Marty released a sigh and left as I picked up the receiver.

"Chief Quick, this is Detective Sergeant Stephanie Fee, Pinellas County Sheriff's Office. Sergeant Roush asked me to give you a call."

"Thank you for responding so quickly, Sergeant."

I passed along the details of the events leading to the discovery at Hannigan's, and mentioned the murder in Clearwater Beach.

"Sounds like the work of a serial killer, Chief."

"I hate to say it, but I agree."

"Have you contacted Clearwater P.D.?"

"No, I…Sergeant, I'm still not certain there's a connection."

"I understand, but at this point I think we should make them aware that the possibility exists."

"Well, okay, Sergeant, but you should know that I'm limited here by not having a designated investigator. My men and I are doing the best we can. I'll be glad to send you what little information we have."

"I appreciate that, Chief, but we can get the reports from the database."

Of course, I thought, remembering my days in Miami.

"I *would* like to see any personal notation you have."

"I'll get it right to you," I said.

"If you'll notify Chief Siddons, I'll get in touch with Clearwater P.D. and we'll make this a concerted effort."

"Works for me."

"Chief, what's *your* take on this guy?"

"He's bold, calculating, and efficient. He acts at times when he could easily get caught. Diversions cover his killings, and to my knowledge, no evidence has been found."

"Sergeant Roush tells me he wouldn't have found our vic if you hadn't been there. By the way, her name is Hannah McClatchy."

"Just playing a hunch, Sergeant. I heard the sirens and thought it was a fire. Which reminds me, this guy used fire here and in Indian Rocks. An argument and gunfire was reported in Clearwater. That's why I have my doubts."

"And in Hidden Rocks Beach he used a bar fight. Interesting also is that he's all over the beach towns and kills in different ways."

"My thoughts exactly, Sergeant."

"Thanks, Chief, and stay in touch."

"Sergeant, there *is* one other thing." Lowering my voice, I said, "A man named Seth Russell *might* be a person of interest."

"Might be?"

"I saw him leaving Hanningan's shortly before we found the body."

"Why are you interested in Russell?"

"He's dating my administrative assistant. I ran into them at our seafood festival on Saturday, and something about him got me to thinking. Call it a gut feeling."

"I'll go see him immediately."

My stomach tightened. "I'd prefer you dig deeper into his background for now. I have a dinner invitation this week where I'm hoping to learn more about him."

"Is it a good idea to wait? If we can tie him to at least

one of the murders, we'll have *something*."

"I understand, but I'm asking you to wait."

"Okay, as long as *you're* the one to answer for this decision if there's another murder."

"I accept that responsibility. And I'd prefer we keep this between us."

"You can *count* on it."

I knew she wasn't happy with the arrangement. I didn't particularly care for it, either.

Putting aside one's duties for personal reasons can bring harsh consequences. Compounded with another murder, I could wind up being branded for life.

I found myself free from disturbance and took the next couple of hours to pore over my notes. A review of the reports, and those I'd received from Siddons and Fee, failed to suggest any kind of lead. A sad fact was staring me in the face. I was stumped. A nagging voice in my head was suggesting that our cases had gone cold. Marty saved the day.

"Eldon, Sam has called three times. He's beyond agitated."

"Guess I'd better humor him."

"When?"

Not only did her assertiveness blindside me, but I felt it was unnecessary.

"Right now."

She turned around then hesitated.

"Is there something else?"

Spinning on her heels, she lowered her head and walked to my desk.

"Eldon, sometimes you make me *so* mad."

"I don't mean to."

"When you ask me questions and don't explain

yourself, it drives me crazy!"

"I'll try not to do it again."

"And that! When you do *that*, it's so frustrating!"

"Do what?"

"*That*! Short, choppy sentences! No feeling. No expression."

"Sorry."

"You did it again!" She caught herself and froze. "I...oh, Eldon, what am I doing? I can't believe I'm yelling at you. I mean, you help me with my problems, and listen when I need to vent. Now I'm standing here yelling at you. I don't know what's happening to me."

I had a good idea of what she was experiencing, but kept it to myself.

"Aren't you going to say anything?" she pleaded.

"I will if you promise not to yell."

"I promise."

"You're in love."

"What! No, I'm not!"

"Okay, you're not. What night do you want me over for dinner?"

Marty hesitated. I knew what she was thinking.

"Wednesday. Is Wednesday a good night for you?"

"Wednesday is fine. What time?"

"Seven."

"Seven, it is."

Without saying another word she turned around and headed for the door. She stopped halfway and looked over her shoulder. "Don't forget to call Sam."

"Doing it now."

"You know, Eldon, sometimes you scare me."

•• ELEVEN ••

COINCIDENCE IS A BELIEF to which some adhere. Thinking of someone or something, only to have the subject appear immediately afterward has been cause for many to wonder. How did it happen? What does it mean? Am I psychic? Whether one chooses to accept it or not, coincidence can sometimes prove interesting.

For me, I choose to believe things happen for a reason. One door closes while another door opens, and the like. More often than not the reason is obvious, whether obscured beforehand or delayed in coming. I'd never found myself without an explanation until Wednesday morning when I took a seat in front of the town council.

The call from Sam was concerning my yearly evaluation. The exercise usually held no suspense or political ramifications, "going through the motions" a more apt description.

The council of three held court, expressed their likes and dislikes, then patted me on the head or wagged their fingers. Usually *a job well done* was the reward. However, I did get a bonus one year, much to the chagrin of Sam Hackney, the lone dissenter.

This day, a trio of glum faces stared across the table leaving me to wonder if their demeanor would be an omen for the entire meeting.

Sam bulled through the evaluation with little or no comment. The others, Kay Little and Rocco Vinelli, nodded in agreement or remained silent. I sensed the tension, but kept a tight rein on my composure. I had a pretty good idea of what was on their minds.

"If you'll just sign at the bottom, El. We've one more topic we wish to discuss with you," Sam said.

I penned my signature and slid the document back to him.

"Now, it's been close to a month since—"

"Sam," Kay Little interrupted. She placed a hand on his forearm. "Eldon, we've been inundated with calls about the unfortunate events that have occurred here and in nearby communities. We know you're doing your best, but we owe it to the residents to ask you for an update on your progress."

Kay reminded me of a grandmother offering a tray of freshly baked cookies. A passel lay before you, but you knew she meant only one. She must have been a first-rate educator ruling the classroom with a temperate hand. She was a master of control without being oppressive. Her manner was so inoffensive. I almost felt like apologizing.

I hesitated, unsure if the council's comprehension of everything surrounding an investigation would be enough to deal with the truth.

"Kay, I purposely withheld going public with our

findings for fear of the effect it would have on the community. I'm not going to mislead you into thinking we're close to catching the perpetrator. At this point, other agencies are involved. And yes, we *are* doing our best to bring closure."

"So the other murders *are* associated with what happened here?" Rocco Vinelli asked.

"Rocco, all I can say is the possibility exists."

"A serial killer!" Sam shouted.

I narrowed my eyes. "Sam, that's exactly the kind of response I'm trying to avoid. What people choose to believe is their business. But *we* don't need to stir the pot." I noticed Sam's jaw tighten.

"Who else is involved in this investigation?" Kay asked.

"Right now, Indian Rocks Beach and the sheriff's office."

"Right now? What do you mean *right now*?" Sam said.

"We're monitoring an incident in Clearwater. We hope to know more in the near future."

"And what are *you* doing...*specifically*?"

"Get off his back, Sam!" Rocco barked. "The man is doing his job to the best of his ability!"

"Why don't we all take a moment to calm down," Kay said. "Eldon can't give us the specific details of an ongoing investigation, and it's unfair of us to pressure him."

"But what am I supposed to tell people when they ask?" Sam said. "The public has a right to know."

"You sound like an ad for a magazine, Sam," Rocco said. "And the public *doesn't* need to know. Eldon's right, it would only cause people to panic."

Kay took the logical road. "What *we* should tell them

is that all efforts are being made to find the one responsible, and voice our full support for Eldon and his staff."

"That's nothing more than a political dodge," Sam grumbled.

Kay turned to him and smiled. "No, Sam, it's the truth. And if anyone can sell the truth, it's you."

Thank you, Kay, I thought.

"She's right, Sam. If we show any doubt, the residents will lose faith in Eldon *and* us," Rocco added.

I allowed Sam some time to think, something he rarely did before opening his mouth. It worked.

"Okay…I'll go along…for now."

Kay smiled.

Rocco shook his head.

I placed an elbow on the table and leaned forward. "I might as well bring this up while I'm here. With the retirement of Glenn Kicklighter six months ago, I'm still down a patrolman." Pausing, I smiled at Kay. "Or woman." Shooting a quick glance at Sam, I continued, "It was supposed to be brought up at the last budget meeting, but—"

"We've had other, more pressing items on the agenda," Sam said.

"I understand, and so far, we've been able to manage, but with vacations coming up, not to mention sick days and personal leave, it's putting a strain on my staff."

"I thought *you* were covering those days?"

"I can only do so much."

"We have to keep an eye on the budget. People are already clamoring about the increase."

"I hear you're thinking of hiring an assistant for Betty."

"No final decision has been made," Rocco said.

His tone of voice told me he was against it.

I was in dire need of another officer, so I wasn't about

to rock the boat by pressing the issue of the assistant to the town manager needing an assistant. Or remind the council that Betty was Sam's niece. Still, I had to make my point.

"Just the same, I'm asking you, all of you, to strongly consider the needs of your police department."

Collective silence was their response. True politicians all.

I thanked them and left.

I felt a bit uncomfortable when I walked into the office. The council did have the right to know about the progress of the investigation. After all, they were the ones fielding the questions. But telling Sam even the vaguest of details amounted to posting them on a social network. I hoped that somehow Kay and Rocco could bridle his tendency to blab.

"Eldon, Sergeant Stephanie Fee called. She said it was urgent."

"Thanks, Marty…and no interruptions until after I speak to her."

"Yes, sir. How'd the meeting go?"

"Oh, you know the usual dog and pony show."

"Are we getting another patrolman?"

"I mentioned it."

"How was it received?"

"It'll be taken into consideration."

"Eldon, the position is already in the budget. What's the holdup?"

I strode into my office and closed the door behind me. Collapsing into my chair, I stared at the phone on my desk.

Better get to it, I thought.

Sergeant Fee answered before the second ring. Although calm, a noticeable edge lined her voice.

"Chief, I've discovered something I'd like to discuss with you."

"I'm all ears," I said.

"What are you doing for lunch?"

"I…really hadn't thought about it."

"Can you pull away and meet me at the Crawford Family Restaurant in half an hour?"

My stomach did a quick flip. The Crawford Family Restaurant boasted the best prices in the county, their food being the reason—roadkill on a plate.

"See you then."

My curiosity was building and caused my right leg to start bouncing up and down. Whatever information Sergeant Fee possessed must have been very important for her not to want to discuss it on the phone.

I grinned. *Or maybe she just wants to get out of the office.*

In a second, my mind turned, and I began to process the data I'd accumulated. A revival of the feeling that I'd missed something was accompanied by an annoying internal voice intent upon wounding my pride. In Miami, I'd been quick to pounce on the smallest of details, seldom passing over the not-so-obvious. Being out of practice, I'd quite possibly overlooked a clue. I glanced at my watch and rose to leave.

"Marty, I have a lunch date. I don't know when I'll be back."

"Okay. Don't forget, my place at seven o'clock tonight."

"Got it."

•• TWELVE ••

AS I ENTERED CRAWFORD'S, I was attacked by the aroma of something resembling beef tips and noodles. Familiar with their "seat yourself" policy, I paused to scan the room, locking onto a pair of attractive women seated in a booth.

The blonde looked up and did a double-take when she saw the uniform. Both of them smiled as I neared. The brunette relocated to the side of the blonde, allowing me a seat across from them.

"I'm Detective Sergeant Stephanie Fee," the blonde said, and extended her right hand. "And this is Detective Sandy Baker."

"A pleasure."

"You're probably wondering why I suggested we meet here."

"The thought crossed my mind."

She shot a glance at her partner. "Sandy and I just *had* to get out of the office."

I chuckled and nodded.

After a brief pause to place our orders, Fee went right to work.

"Chief, we beat our brains out going over the reports and other information, and were growing frustrated by the minute. There wasn't anything there to connect the murders. Then we saw it on the autopsy reports, actually Sandy did. They all had a similar tattoo."

I grimaced and shook my head.

"Something wrong, Chief?"

"I always look like this when I miss something."

Mullen and Jarvis had several tattoos. I'd seen the notations in the reports, but paid little attention to them. Why would I? Tattoos were very common.

"We researched the tat and found it to be a Chinese symbol for unity. Mullen had one on his neck. Jarvis, on her ankle. Jbara, on his shoulder. And McClatchy, on her right breast." She handed me a folder. "McClatchy, no arrest record."

I pulled my chin a couple of times thinking about all of the victims. "Different professions, different social classes, different genders, same epidermal graffiti. I can't imagine what would draw these people together."

"Epidermal graffiti?"

"Tattoos. I'm not a big fan."

Fee glanced at Baker.

"We don't see it either, Chief."

"And this tattoo is the symbol for *unity*?"

"There are many styles and interpretations," Baker said. "This particular tat is in the Kaiti style."

"Good work, Detective."

Fee covered her mouth and did her best not to laugh.

"Did I say something wrong?"

"No, Chief, it's just that…Sandy has a lotus blossom

on her back."

"Stevie, you didn't have to tell him that!"

"Well, I guess that makes you our expert." To Fee, I asked, "Is that what your friends call you…Stevie?"

"Yeah," she said, and looked down.

"Her former partner gave her that nickname," Baker said.

Thinking I'd stuck my foot in my mouth, I tried to recover. "He must have thought a great deal of you."

Fee looked up with serious eyes. "He was the best."

"Sorry, Sergeant, I didn't mean to pry."

"Chief, it's not you. It's just…a few years ago we were working a case, and he wound up getting shot. He retired shortly after. I never quite got over…"

The name of her partner became as clear as the pain on her face.

"You were Lance Newbern's sidekick. The man who shook up Seminole Beach."

She nodded.

"How's he doing?"

The glimmer of a smile reversed her mood.

"He's doing good. He's always teasing me about how much he enjoys retirement. I try to see him as often as I can." She looked down again, the glimmer fading.

"Sergeant…Stevie…I used to work Homicide in Miami. I lost my partner in a shootout. I think about him every day. Believe me, Lance doesn't want you feeling the way you do."

"I know, but if I had just…"

"Stevie, you can't change the past. You can only do your best right now, today." I sat back. "So let's put our heads together and try to catch this guy."

Stevie snapped her head up with her eyes narrowed. "We *will* catch him!"

I stared at her a second, then at Baker.

"Chief, when she gets this way, the best thing you can do is fasten your seat belt and hang on."

· · THIRTEEN · ·

SERGEANT FEE'S INTENSITY and fierce desire gave me a lot to think about on my trip back to the office. She radiated a need for success, not in the spotlight, but for self-satisfaction. Her determination and apparent motivation were admirable—*and* a warning. Such strong will can result in alienation from those around a person. Not to mention it can ruin relationships. A good many people pull away from the driven, not understanding and feeling disassociated. I suspected Fee's social life, if she had one, suffered at the hands of her obsession, and imagined her alone in retirement wondering if it all had been worth it.

Not a good place to be, I thought, and retrieved my cell phone.

"Marty, I'm heading home. I've had enough for one day."

"You're still coming tonight, aren't you?"

"Of course."

I heard her exhale.

"Good, I thought you might be sick or something."

"No, Crawford's has a few things that don't disagree with me."

"Crawford's? Why on earth did you go there?"

"Not my call."

"Somebody really must have it in for you."

"Nah, more like a half-way point."

"But, Eldon…Crawford's? There are plenty of restaurants your date could have

chosen."

"She wasn't my date. It was strictly a business lunch. You want me there at eight, right?"

"Eldon, I said seven! Please don't embarrass me tonight."

"Would I do that? I bought a brand new pink Hawaiian shirt for the occasion. It goes perfect with my green plaid shorts and red socks."

Silence filled my ear.

"You *are* joking, right?"

I waited, resisting the urge to laugh. "Of course I'm joking. See you at seven."

"Oooh, sometimes you are so infuriating!"

I released my laughter and ended the call, picturing Marty as a teenager teeming with anxiety whenever her father held court with her dates.

My mood changed quickly when the thought of the tattoo entered my mind. Somehow, a seemingly unrelated group of people were tied together. And the tattoo was the link.

Marty answered the door before the last chime faded. With a wide-eyed look of uncertainty, she gave me a quick going-over. Then she began to breathe again.

"Whew, you had me worried."

"Now, Marty, I thought you knew me better than that."

Secretly, I was happy my blue, hibiscus-laden Hawaiian shirt didn't offend her.

She invited me inside. "I like your shirt," she whispered. "And thank you for wearing your tan slacks instead of the plaid shorts."

I smiled, knowing the slacks were covering my blazing red socks.

"Why don't you join Seth on the sofa and I'll get you a beer. Dinner's almost ready."

"What's on the menu?"

"Baked chicken, mashed potatoes, and green beans."

Marty knew I couldn't get enough chicken. Preparing it in any fashion won me over.

Seth was lounging on the sofa in a manner suggesting total reassurance. He didn't bother to stand when I approached.

"Chief, long time, no see."

"Good to see you again, Seth."

His body language implied self-confidence bordering on cockiness. A white, short-sleeved Chambray shirt, dark blue cargo shorts, and bright white Nike sneakers without socks told me his quest to secure Marty's friendship had been successful. No doubt he was entertaining thoughts of them living together in the near future.

"How's the criminal business going?" he asked. "Marty tells me it's been quiet lately."

"For the most part."

"No bad guys disrupting the tranquility of your little town?"

"Not at the moment."

"That's good to hear. Deemer's Inlet is so picturesque and peaceful. It'd be a shame if some outside influence caused a disruption."

Something about the tone and inflection of his voice hit me wrong.

To many born and raised in Florida, *anyone* from outside the state was a tourist—and always would be. I kept an open mind on the subject, allowing a person's actions to guide my judgment.

"I'm not sure many *outside influences*, as you put it, even know that Deemer's Inlet exists. We're a well-kept secret in these parts."

His laughter complemented his condescending manner. This guy believed my town to be *Podunkville*.

"Here's your beer," Marty said, and took a chair nearby.

She sat up straight, alert, watching for any signs of discord between Seth and me.

"Oh, Chief, before I forget, I had a wonderful time at the seafood festival. It reminds me of the county fairs in the Midwest."

"It's a nice change of pace. Besides helping the local businesses, it's an extra source of revenue."

"Ah, yes, revenue. The underlying motive for all things."

I grinned. "A sad fact of life, actually. And you know politicians. They always have that bottom line on their minds."

"Ain't it the truth? The mayor seems like a nice fellow, though. He certainly is proud of himself."

"Sam's okay, he just has his own ideas on how to run things."

"Dinner will be ready in five minutes," Marty said, and left for the kitchen.

I seized the moment. "Seth, you mentioned the Midwest. Is that where you've always lived?"

"Pretty much. My job has taken me other places, but mostly the Midwest."

"Sales can be a tough occupation, especially in these times."

"You're telling me. I enjoy it, though. One thing I learned early on is you have to grab an opportunity when it arises. No other way to the big money, if you know what I mean."

"Sounds too competitive for me."

"It's *very* competitive. I have to be on my game every day. And talk about the bottom line. My boss is on my ass all the time. And the stress, oh…my god, sometimes it's unbearable. But you know, Chief, I wouldn't have it any other way." He took a swig of beer and smiled. "Does that make me a masochist?"

"Not in my mind. I'd say you were success oriented. Looking for a better station in life. Nothing wrong with that."

He leaned forward. "I like you, Chief. You're a man of few words, but you say a lot. If you were my competition, I'd be worried."

I took a healthy pull of beer and sat back. "Seth, you don't strike me as a man who worries about much. I'll bet you've been successful everywhere you've been."

He threw his hands up, palms out. "You got me, Chief, take me in!" He released that staccato, cartoonish laughter again. "But really, it's the challenge that excites me…the bigger, the better."

I smiled. *And if you hurt Marty, I'll crush you*, I

thought. "I'm curious though, Seth. If you're motivated by the hunt, why Florida? Why Tampa Bay? I would think New York or Los Angeles would be more attractive."

He offered a cocky smile. "Don't misunderstand me, Chief. This area is everything I could want. But every so often I take a break. Sometimes, it's nice not to have to go full-tilt into every day just to survive."

"You don't take vacations?"

"I play as hard as I work. I know how to relax. I'm talking about cruising instead of accelerating."

I nodded.

Cruising instead of accelerating was fine as long as the bills got paid. Not knowing his money-handling capability, I could only assume that he made the correct adjustments to prepare for those periods. But being young *and* successful, he most likely lived according to his ways and means. And maybe above. The likelihood of there being a safety net didn't seem probable, so another avenue of income must exist.

Then again, I might be wrong, I thought.

"Dinner's ready," Marty sang out.

Seth grinned before he stood up. "Is she a good cook?"

"Only my wife was better."

The rest of the evening proved to be an exercise in mindless babble.

I learned nothing more of Seth other than his idea of fun, his taste in clothes, and his feelings toward Marty.

"Chief, you're really lucky to have her on your staff. I can tell by the way she handles herself that she's very efficient at her job."

"Make no mistake, Seth, *she* runs the department. I just get the credit."

I found it odd that he lacked curiosity in regard to police work. Most people have an endless supply of questions and aren't shy about asking. Seth seemed content to talk about anything but, and like Sam Hackney, proved to be very proud of himself.

Around eleven o'clock, I'd grown tired of his act, so I thanked Marty and bowed out.

My ride home would take about twenty minutes, enough time to review and make an assessment of him. My cell phone disrupted the plan.

"Chief, its Barney."

Immediately I thought the worst. Barney never called unless it was absolutely necessary.

"Barney, what's wrong?"

Relax, Chief, nothin's wrong. Look, I was thinkin', the shift change's due soon and maybe I could give ya a hand. If ya need it, I mean."

"I appreciate the offer, but after working a full day you'll be too tired."

"Aw, Chief, I don't mind. Ya got your hands full runnin' the department and dealin' with the council. That don't give ya much time fer investigatin'."

"How does Sue Ellen feel about it?"

Barney chuckled. "We have us a understandin'. She don't ask, and I don't tell. Besides, Bo's goin' on vacation in two weeks, so you'll be coverin' fer him anyways. We can team up if ya need ta check somethin' out."

I'd completely forgotten about Bo's being gone. Having Barney along to go over the crime scenes and hash things out would be a plus.

"All right, Barney, but only if it's necessary. You know how the council feels about overtime."

"I ain't askin' fer no overtime. I want ta help ya."

"I couldn't ask you to do that on your own time. I wouldn't feel right."

"Well, whatever ya decide is fine by me. How'd the meetin' go?"

"I got my annual 'pat-on-the-head.' But they're worried about the murders. I guess they've been getting a lot of phone calls."

"Yeah, I figgered by now ol' Sam'd be throwin' wood on the cookin' fire ta roast your butt. He just don't get it."

"And never will. How's it going tonight?"

"All quiet on the western front, so ta speak."

"Good, and thanks, Barney. Say, why'd you wait so late to call?"

"I knew you was goin' ta Marty's, and figgered you'd be headin' home 'bout now."

"Are you sure you're not a mind reader?"

"Naw, Chief, I just pays attention."

"Oh, I just remembered. You're familiar with some of the tattoo parlors around the area, right? Where would someone go to get a Chinese symbol?"

"Pert near all of 'em. They's popular with the younger guys and gals."

"Get with me tomorrow and I'll fill you in."

"Does this have ta do with the murders?"

"Yes, but I didn't tell you that."

"There's only a coupla places ol' Mullet and Lucy Jarvis could afford ta go. After ya tell me more, I'll go ta them places first."

"Works for me. And Barney, we never had this conversation, okay?"

"What conversation, Chief?"

The sound of his laughter was the perfect end to my evening.

• • FOURTEEN • •

THE NEXT MORNING I CALLED the office when I knew Marty would be there. A gut feeling awakened me and I wanted to tend to it as soon as possible.

"Eldon, are you all right?" Marty asked.

"Of course. I need to check on a couple of things, so I'll be in later."

"Oh, thank God. I thought you might have gotten sick."

"You worry about me too much."

"Of course I worry about you. I worry about the others, too…and I thought maybe something you ate might not have agreed with you."

"Well now that you mention it, those mashed potatoes did sit down kind of heavy."

"Really? I thought I used enough…oh, Eldon!"

I couldn't help laughing. Marty's whirlwind romance really had her shook up, though I couldn't say the same for Seth.

"Everything was delicious. And I enjoyed talking to

Seth," I lied.

"He likes you, too. He went on and on about how you put things into perspective so concisely. He calls it *subtle strength*."

Overkill to get on your good side, I thought. *And I'm not so sure the feeling is mutual.* "Any calls?"

"One, from Rocco Vinelli. He wants to meet with you today."

"I'll call him when I get in."

"I would like a few minutes of your time, too…if that's all right."

"I *always* have time for you, Marty."

"Good. It's nothing important, really."

I'd been around Marty long enough to know that *nothing important* meant *personal*.

"Is it about Seth?"

"Well…why don't you like him? I know you said you did, but…I get the feeling you don't."

"Why would you think I don't like him?"

"You have certain tendencies when you're interrogating someone."

"I wasn't interrogating him."

She sighed. "Eldon, some people may be fooled by your relaxed style, but I know when you're trying to pry information out of someone."

"Marty, we were just talking."

"Are you *sure*?"

"Sure we were talking? Of course."

"Eldon don't make fun of me. I'm serious."

I could see where this was heading and now wasn't the right time to list my concerns.

"We'll talk when I get in."

"Okay, I'm going to hold you to it."

I'd taken to Marty my first day on the job. Call it a hunch, but I felt she needed a little guidance even as she approached her late twenties. And maybe guidance wasn't the correct term. Without a doubt she was her father's daughter. Maybe acceptance better described her need.

I chuckled when I saw Barney's patrol car sitting in the parking lot of the Happy Clam motel. Waiting to hear his excuse for being there made pleasurable my short walk to the beach behind the business.

"Howdy, Chief, what brings *you* here?"

"The same thing that brought you here, I imagine."

He grinned and shook his head. "Right minds think alike."

"I still think you're a mind reader."

"Chief, somethin' 'bout ol' Mullet bein' here just never seemed right ta me. It coulda been drugs. He was known ta howl at the moon on occasion. But outside of findin' a place ta sleep, he didn't wander too far from the docks."

"You think he was lured here?"

"Yep. And it musta been somethin' big."

"You think he came here to *sell* drugs as opposed to buying them?"

"Coulda been, but he ain't got no car. He woulda had ta found some other way. And there ain't many who liked 'im enough ta haul 'im around."

Barney was Deemer's Inlet's version of CSI. I'd take his observations over the most scientific of analyses.

"So, what's your hunch?"

"I don't know, Chief. He weren't smart enough for

no sophisticated jobs. If somebody else was callin' the shots then maybe." Barney winced and tilted his head to the side. "But askin' ol' Mullet fer help'd be rollin' the dice."

"Maybe that's what got him killed. Maybe he crossed the wrong person."

Barney nodded and reached into his pants pocket. "And maybe *this* belongs ta that person." He handed me an evidence bag containing a pendant and gold chain.

The pendant was a little larger than a quarter with decorative etchings around the edge. Nothing special about the design, and may have been worn by a man *or* a woman.

"Where'd you find this?"

"In the sand, close ta where we found 'im. If the sun hadn't hit it just right, I'd never seen it."

"Looks expensive."

"Maybe, but one thing's fer sure. It don't belong ta ol' Mullet.

Although Barney was right about the pendant, I couldn't be certain that someone didn't drop it before Mullen's murder—or after.

"Now tell me 'bout them tattoos."

• • FIFTEEN • •

MARTY GREETED ME with a quick glance, a short "hello," and didn't offer a cup of coffee. Recalling the same treatment directed at Reed Logan when he once made an off-handed remark, I figured I'd better deal with her sooner rather than later.

"Something wrong, Marty?"

"Nope, everything's just peachy."

"You're not acting like it."

She snapped her head up. "I just can't believe you don't like Seth!"

"I never said I didn't like him."

"You don't have to. I can tell."

I leaned down and placed both hands on her desk. "What's bothering you more, that I have reservations or that I remind you of your father?"

"Don't bring my father into this! You have no right! You're not giving Seth a chance! That's what bothering me!"

I straightened up. "Let's go into my office and talk

about it."

Her eyes softened and the strained lines in her forehead eased. "No, Rocco called again. We'll talk after you're done with him."

I went to my desk and sat down. Marty was right. I wasn't giving Seth a chance. I had my reasons—legitimate reasons as far as I was concerned.

I picked up the phone and called Rocco.

"Eldon, thanks for getting back to me. There's something I want to run by you. Can we meet somewhere?"

Uh-oh, another personal agenda item, I thought. "Rocco, I've got a lot going on today. Could we discuss it on the phone?"

"Well, sure…and just so you know, I'm against hiring an assistant for Betty. She *does* have a lot on her plate, but if she didn't take so many cigarette breaks she'd get more accomplished. You know how Sam feels, and Kay is undecided. Sometimes I think she enjoys walking the fence just to torture us. Anyhoo, *if* we vote in favor of another police officer, I have a candidate I'd like you to consider."

"And who might that be?"

"My daughter. Now before you say anything, please hear me out. Francesca and her husband moved here two months ago from Ocala. She has six years' experience with the Ocala Police Department. He got a better job offer in Tampa, but neither of them wants to live there."

"Has she applied to other agencies?"

"Yes, but she's still waiting to hear from them."

"Rocco, I'm not a big fan of nepotism. I've seen it cause too many problems in the past."

"I understand, Eldon, and I wouldn't want any

preferential treatment. But her record is exemplary. Check it out, you'll see. All I'm asking you to do is give her a shot."

Favoritism exists in every level of government, make no mistake about it. In small towns, though, favoritism seems to thrive, unavoidable in some instances, I suppose. Deemer's Inlet was not one of those towns. And *no one* was going to point an accusing finger at me.

"Have her stop by and fill out an application, Rocco. But I'm telling you up front, I'm hiring the applicant with the best qualifications. Man or woman, I don't care. Whoever is best suited will get the job."

"Thanks, Eldon, I appreciate it. And if you ever need any brick work done, give me a call. I'll do you right."

You've got to love politicians. The man says he wants no special considerations, but tosses in a bribe anyway.

Maybe I'll take him up on his offer. A wall ten-foot high around my office just might be the way to go.

I was about to call Marty in when I heard the phone ring. Not more than a minute later she appeared in the doorway.

"Sergeant Fee is on line one."

She paused only to watch me pick up the receiver.

"Chief, have you had a chance to go over the report I gave you?" Fee asked.

"No, I just got in."

"Hannah McClatchy, no middle name, is a legal secretary for the offices of Leventhal and Rand in Tampa."

I'd forgotten and left the folder in my SUV, so I scribbled down the information thinking another connection may be falling into place. Tampa.

"Age twenty-eight, born in Brandon, lived in Pinellas Park, and no criminal record...oh, yes, I told you that."

"Wonder what she was doing in a place like Hannigan's?" I said.

"Are you sure she was there?"

"Just thinking out loud."

"Right now her murder appears to be coincidental in regards to the others."

"I agree, Sergeant. I have something else you'll find interesting. Hold on." Laying down the receiver, I rose and closed the office door before returning to my desk. "One of my men found some evidence at the first murder location. It's a small pendant on a gold chain."

"Really! What do you make of it?"

"Too expensive for the victim. I think the killer lost it."

"I'd like to have a look at it."

"You read my mind, Sergeant. I'd be grateful if you'd take it to your lab."

"We'll get the results quicker, too. No offense."

"None taken. If luck smiles on us, maybe we'll come up with a fingerprint or two."

"That would be awesome! Chief, if you don't mind my asking, how is it this pendant was missed the first time?"

"Two reasons. First, we found the victim at night. We're not equipped for a major homicide investigation. Second, the pendant was buried in sugar sand, easy to miss. The officer happened to catch a reflection from the morning sun when he went back to look around."

"Buy that man a beer."

"I'll run it right up to you."

"Listen, Chief...about yesterday...I appreciate everything you said. You were right about Lance not wanting me to feel guilty. When he left that night, I didn't want him to go alone. And normally he wouldn't, but he got so caught up in what was happening that he wouldn't listen to me. He could be real stubborn at times."

"Like his partner?"

I heard her laugh.

"I guess it rubbed off on me."

"Sergeant, do you like chicken?"

"What?"

"Do *you* like chicken?"

"Sure, I eat it once in a while."

"I was thinking of throwing some on the grill tonight. Care to join me?"

The next few seconds of silence told me I'd blundered—or she was thinking.

"I appreciate your offer, but honestly it's kind of weird."

"Not meant to be. Please accept my apology. I have a few theories bouncing around in my head. There's no one here with your experience to share them. But I understand your reluctance."

"Is this about your dispatcher's boyfriend?"

"Now you've got it."

"What time should I be there? And what can I bring?"

"Eight o'clock and your thinking cap will do nicely."

The real reason Fee called made me like her even more. And in truth, I *did* need a sounding board to air my suspicions. She met the criteria and more. Plus, she would have an opportunity to relax, something in which, I suspect, she had little practice. I rose and walked to the door.

"Marty, let's talk now."

Marty entered my office without saying a word, and

took a seat in front of my desk. I began slowly. "You're right. I haven't been fair with Seth. And before you get all worked up, you should know it's because I'm concerned about you, friend-to-friend. I know it's none of my business, but you just broke up with that other guy. I don't want to see you get hurt again."

I could see the fight in her diminishing.

"And here I was all set for an argument. I appreciate your caring about me, Eldon. I'm sure a lot of people wish they had friends like you. You're right, though, Seth and I *are* moving too fast. Sometimes it scares me, especially when he drops little hints about us living together."

Bingo! I thought.

"I know I'm partly to blame. I want a relationship. A permanent relationship. Sometimes I dream about how great it would be. Other times, I'm not so sure."

"Go on."

"Seth has been really nice to me, generous even, but there have been a couple of times when he…" A look bordering the edge of uncertainty covered her face. "Eldon, after we saw you at the festival, I was ready for a night alone with him. We went to my place, kicked back with some wine, and began to talk. I was in heaven. Everything was falling into place. Suddenly, he gets this phone call. I didn't mind so much that he didn't want to talk in front of me, but after he hung up, he apologized and left. He said he would explain later. He never did."

"Did you ask him?"

"I didn't want to come off as overly possessive."

"Has this happened before?"

"Oh, he gets work-related calls all the time. I can see where it might become a problem, but he usually doesn't leave."

"How many times has he left?"

"Three, so far."

Another woman.

"What do *you* think?"

"You're not going to like what I'm about to say."

"Oh, please, don't tell me there's someone else."

Mind readers! I'm surrounded by mind readers! "Maybe you and Seth should take a break. Tell him the truth. Tell him you believe the relationship is moving too fast, and you need some time to think. If he's *really* interested, he'll understand."

"What if he doesn't understand? What if he doesn't come back? I don't want to go through that all over again."

"Okay, let me ask you this: if he moves in, and down the road you discover it's not working out, are you going to feel any worse about his leaving than you would now?"

Marty pinched up her face and rocked her head from side to side. "Oh, I don't know. Why does this have to be so complicated? What should I do, Eldon?"

"You have to decide that for yourself."

She stood up slowly with her head lowered. "I think I would have preferred our yelling at one another."

"Not good to make decisions when you're upset."

"Stop sounding like my father, will you?"

"I'll try."

"No you won't."

• • SIXTEEN • •

THE AFTERNOON TURNED OUT to be nice and quiet, opening the door for an uneventful ride to the sheriff's office. Dropping off the pendant to Sergeant Fee, I cut short my visit and headed west on Ulmerton Road.

A return to Deemer's Inlet along the coast pushed aside the morning's mental gymnastics. Not to say that I was ignoring Rocco's lobby or Marty's predicament. I simply wanted some alone time to think.

My suspicion of Seth was growing by the minute. Not so much his interaction with Marty as his being at Hannigan's. Two months in new surroundings provided plenty of time for an intelligent person to acclimate, especially if the way was paved beforehand. But I wasn't buying Seth's assertion that he took positions requiring less effort as a means of stress relief. While I appreciated someone with ambition, bouncing around from job to job could also mean getting out while the getting was good. Translation: disappearing before some sharp detective caught on.

The unexplained phone calls added mystery to the quick exits Marty observed. Having her worried another woman had entered the picture was a perfect cover for other undertakings. If she complained, he could apologize, saying he didn't want to bore her with the menial tasks of his work. Or, as she noted, he could assume an adversarial pose, claiming she was becoming too possessive and end the relationship. He'd already displayed the ability to read people, and I suspected his calculating mind concocted avenues of escape long before he approached a candidate. Blessed with a gregarious personality, and a quick though forced smile, Seth could easily manipulate people, thereby creating the means to his personal goal—a goal yet to be revealed.

Another item of note I found interesting was his casual attire. I'm certain that when on the job he dressed the part of a successful salesman oozing with confidence. During my interactions with him, though, he dressed down—not sloppy or unkempt—more of a *rich kid being cool* approach. Oddly, the usual gold trophies around his neck or on his hands didn't exist. He didn't even wear a watch. I realize the younger generation relies on other means for the time of day, but I would have thought Seth to be a Rolex or Breitling kind of guy. If that were the case, the pendant wouldn't fit unless it figured into his business wardrobe.

Marty seemed to be back to her old self when I walked into the office. I hoped she hadn't made a decision too soon. Hoped she had taken time to think it through before passing the news on to Seth.

"Sam called. He wants to talk to you before you leave today."

I dropped my head. "Marty, do you suppose others

101

in my position have to deal with council members as often as I do? Small town chiefs, I mean?"

"No, Eldon, I think you're one of the chosen."

"That's what I figured."

I sat down at my desk, picked up the receiver, and thought, *I hope he doesn't want an update on the murders.*

"Well, it's about time you called!" Sam barked. "What have you been doing all day?"

"My job, Sam. Now what's so important to get you all rankled?"

"Have you made any headway towards apprehending the serial killer? He's still the top story in the news, but they're just rehashing what happened."

"That should tell you everything."

"That's not good enough! You need to be putting more effort into catching him!"

"How do you know what I'm doing? Or any of the other agencies for that matter? And in case you've forgotten, I'm still short one officer!"

"Don't you throw that in my face! People are crying out for resolve! They want this matter brought to an end!"

"Don't you think I know that! We're doing the best we can!"

"Not good enough! I'm beginning to think we made a mistake when we hired you!"

"Tell you what, Sam, when this is over, you can have my badge!"

I slammed down the receiver and fought the urge to sling the phone across the room.

Marty appeared in the doorway, hesitating before she entered. "You're not *really* going to quit, are you, Eldon?"

I came close to exploding. "I don't appreciate you eavesdropping on my conversations."

"It was hard not to. You know, someone once told me that it's not good to make decisions when you're upset."

I stared hard at her, too angry to speak.

She turned around and left.

At a quarter after four, I had calmed down somewhat, and decided to go home. I wanted plenty of time to put the day behind me and prepare for my evening with Sergeant Fee.

"Getting ready for the big date," Marty teased.

I let go a sigh. "Marty, mind your own business, please."

"She's a little young for you, isn't she?"

The needle was out and the gauntlet thrown.

"And how would you know *that*?"

"By the sound of her voice…and I ran a background check."

"Well, Miss Nosey, for your information, her stopping by is strictly for business purposes."

"Uh-huh."

"Truth is she reminds me a lot of you."

"Really?"

"Yeah, she's stubborn, hard-headed, and at times a real pain in the ass, I'm told."

"Thanks a lot!"

"Think nothing of it." I made a small bow and left.

Chicken on the grill, potatoes in the oven, vegetables

on the stove, I had everything going when Sergeant Fee arrived.

Prompt, a trait worth noting, she appeared uneasy at first, still unsure If I had an underlying motive for the invitation, I'm certain.

"Hi, Chief. Hope I'm not too early."

"Right on time. Please come in."

"Chief, I'm not much of a beer drinker, so I brought some wine."

"How'd you know I drank beer?"

Her smile was warm.

"I'm a detective."

"Okay, first point of order: off the clock my name is Eldon, not Chief."

"That works for me, Eldon."

I opened the bottle of wine, filled a glass, grabbed a brew for myself, and escorted her to the patio. "We're almost ready. Have a seat and relax."

"Eldon, this is beautiful. You'd never know it from the road."

"My secret hideaway. Guaranteed to cure what ails ya."

She eased down onto the pastel yellow lawn chair. "I don't mean to be nosey, but how come you don't have a patio table?"

I took a swig of beer. "I used to when my wife was alive. We ate out here a lot.

She loved this view, too. When she passed away, I don't know. Every time

I saw that table the memories were too strong, so I got rid of it."

"I'm sorry." Stevie swirled her wine then looked up and slowly took in the surroundings. "I need to find a place like this. After I retire, I mean." She took a small sip of her wine.

"I hope you like brussels sprouts. I'm guilty of assuming that everyone does."

Stevie's head snapped up. "I *love* brussels sprouts! I wish more restaurants served them. I'm too lazy to cook them at home."

Tired is more like it, I thought. "Good, then I won't get stuck eating leftovers for a week."

Her laughter was a most pleasant sound.

"I need to check on the chicken."

Stevie jumped up. "Let me give you a hand."

We prepared the dining table and sat down, talking about everything and nothing. So different away from the job, Stevie now seemed right at home, a quick reversal from when she arrived. Whether it was the wine or the atmosphere or both, her tough exterior melted. An attractive young woman emerged, assured yet vulnerable.

"I get too wrapped up in my job. My focus is so intense that nothing else seems to matter."

"Admirable in one sense." I took a healthy pull of beer.

"I suppose, but it hasn't done much for my social life."

"It can be a hindrance."

"I was seeing this guy for a while. I thought he was a great guy. And I thought he understood."

"Only a cop understands. The others just tolerate it."

"Amen to that."

I noticed her empty glass and picked up the bottle.

A grin raised the corners of her mouth.

"Eldon, are you trying to get me drunk?"

"No, ma'am. Just enhancing the relaxation factor."

Her grin widened, and she thanked me.

"You were a detective, weren't you? How did you handle it?"

"I was fortunate to have a wife who went above and beyond. She had an amazing capacity to help me forget the job when I came home. Not all the time, but most of the time."

"What about those other times?"

I shook my head. "I don't know why she stuck around. I was a bear."

"You?"

"You'd never know it by looking at me today, would you?"

Stevie laughed, but quickly dropped her eyes. I knew what she was thinking.

"Stevie, I don't profess to know much, but I do know that when the bell rings and it's time to go home, you have to turn it off. Otherwise…"

"I know. I don't want to burn out, but I don't want to transfer out of Homicide, either."

I rested my arms on the table. "You're a smart woman. You'll figure out what's right for you."

"You think so?"

"If you don't, I'll come off sounding like an idiot. Don't let that happen."

"I'll do my best."

I sat back and folded my arms. "I hate to break this up, but I *did* want to discuss a few things with you."

"Yes! Tell me about the boyfriend."

I related my findings, suspicions, and observations. Stevie sat entranced, processing and retaining, a sponge to my every word. A strange sensation came over me, an excitement I'd known in the past. Conversing with her ignited a spark long since extinguished—or so I believed. I had to contain myself a few times, feeling the same electricity I'd shared with my partner in Miami. My body knew better, but my brain continued to release the energy.

"Eldon, if I was going strictly on what you've told me, I'd arrest this Seth Russell tomorrow."

"That makes two of us."

We stared at one another, no words necessary, because one important piece of the puzzle remained undiscovered—proof.

"How are you going to handle it? With Marty, I mean?"

"A good question, Stevie. Her being involved makes this a delicate situation."

"You're in a tough spot, all right. If you *don't* tell her and you're right, her life could be in danger. If you *do* tell her and you're wrong, she'll hate you for the rest of your life."

I'd faced tough situations before, but never on a close, personal level.

"If you ask me today, I'll take the hate. But tomorrow is another day."

"I hear *that*, but don't wait too long. If we find Russell's fingerprints on the pendant, we've *got* to bring him in. And I should know something by tomorrow." Stevie glanced at her watch. "Holy crap, it's after one!"

"Time flies when you're having fun."

"I'd better be going."

"Stevie, there's one more thing. This is a small town and word travels fast. If it gets out that you were here so late, well, people may get the wrong impression."

"Eldon, my personal life is *my* business. I ain't sayin' nothin' to nobody."

"Good, because I'm more concerned with *who* might hear."

Stevie bat her eyes, dreamy. "If that happens, I suppose we *could* play to their fantasies."

"I'm talking about Seth Russell. He has the means to pick up and leave at the drop of a hat."

"Oh, right. Good point. We'll keep our fingers crossed." An impish grin suddenly appeared. "But if it got out somehow then let them believe what they want to believe."

"Good night, Stevie."

She hesitated at the front door and her playfulness vanished. "Eldon, thanks for inviting me to dinner. And thanks for helping me unwind. I really needed it."

"Any time."

• • SEVENTEEN • •

MARTY SURPRISED ME the next morning by greeting me with a smile brighter than usual, a cup of coffee, and refraining from the bombardment of questions I expected. Prepared to dance around the topics Stevie and I discussed, I accepted the dispensation with silent gratitude.

Moving to my office I prepared for the day, confident this Friday would turn out better than those in recent weeks. Ten minutes later, Marty knocked on my door.

"Eldon, I talked to Seth last night."

"Oh?"

"I told him we needed to take a break."

"What'd he say?"

"He asked me why, and I told him. I told him things were moving too fast, and I needed time to think."

"How'd he react?"

"Surprisingly, he took it well. I thought he'd get upset, but he said he understood."

"Is that all?"

"He admitted that he'd been thinking about it, too, but wasn't sure how I'd feel."

That doesn't sound like Seth, I thought.

Pretenses aside, Seth didn't impress me as one who would shy away from expressing himself. His ego wouldn't allow it.

"How do you feel?"

"I'm okay."

"*Okay* okay, or *okay*, I'm not sure?"

"Actually, I'm feeling very good and I don't know why. Once I got home and settled down, I thought about what you said. I won't tell you I wasn't scared when I called him, but afterward I felt relieved."

"Because he didn't yell or because he understood?"

"Because I think there's another woman."

"The secret phone calls."

"Seth is a salesman, and a good one. I hate to use the word *manipulator*, but I believe he has the skill to talk anyone into doing almost anything."

Well put.

"And when he started hinting around about moving in, I didn't know what to think. Well, maybe I did. Maybe I'm too paranoid because it hasn't worked out in the past."

"And maybe you weren't ready," I said.

"Could be. My friends Leah and Olivia, you've met them, they once told me I came across as desperate. You know, trying too hard. Funny isn't it? I finally meet a guy I think is the right one, and now I'm not so sure."

"At least you had the good sense to step back and think about it."

"No, *you* had the good sense. If I hadn't listened to you I might have found myself in big trouble."

My heart skipped a beat. "Big trouble? What do you mean *big trouble*?"

"There's something mysterious about Seth. I guess I didn't want to admit it when I first met him."

"Marty, that's true of everyone in the beginning."

"That's not what I mean. I've talked his ears off about my family, my friends, about you and the guys, but he hasn't even mentioned anything personal. He's never talked about anyone outside of his job."

"Maybe he's reluctant to open up until he feels more comfortable."

"Why would he be reluctant to talk about his family?"

"Maybe they're an embarrassment to him." I allowed a tight smile to cover my face.

Marty stared at me a second. "What's so funny?"

"I was just thinking how different you are today compared to yesterday."

"It's your fault."

"Of course."

Marty placed both hands on her hips. "So, are you going to tell me or not?"

"Or not."

"Come on, Eldon, the curiosity's killing me."

"Curiosity killed the cat."

"And satisfaction brought him back. Come on, give it up."

I cleared my throat. "Sergeant Fee and I had a dinner of grilled chicken, baked potatoes, and brussels sprouts. Then we—"

"Brussels sprouts! Who eats brussels sprouts? Especially on a date?"

"She happens to like brussels sprouts. And it wasn't a date."

"Weird. Go on."

"She drank wine, I drank beer, and we talked about police work."

"That's it?"

"That's it."

"Right! And I'm quitting my job to become the star performer for Cirque de Soleil."

"Sorry to disappoint you."

She looked at me for the longest of seconds.

"You're not kidding, are you?"

"I'm not kidding, and I'd appreciate your not mentioning this to anyone."

"Oh?"

"Not because of what you're thinking, Marty. Certain people don't need to know."

The seriousness of my request finally hit her.

"Someone we know is a suspect?"

The telephone came to my rescue. Marty glanced over her shoulder then back to me. I nodded, and she scurried off, no doubt consumed with frustration.

About to tackle some overdue paperwork, I looked up when I heard Charlie Bates and Reed Logan enter my office.

"If you're bucking for a raise by coming in early, I can't help you."

Charlie laughed. Reed smiled.

"No, Chief, nothing like that," Charlie said.

"Although it would be nice if you mentioned it to the town council," Reed said.

I gave him a tight smile. "What's on your minds?"

"Chief, you know we start the night shift next week. Well, Reed and I...we'd like to swap sectors...if that's okay with you."

"Sure, and if you decide to change back, that's okay, too."

Reed glanced at Charlie when he began shifting in place. "Chief, being the newest member on the force, I didn't feel it was my place to make such a request. The truth is I'm bored with patrolling the north sector. I mentioned it to Charlie, and he thought we should check with you first."

"It's not a problem. And in the future, you don't need to ask permission. As long as we're covered, I don't mind."

They both nodded, but didn't move.

"Something else?"

Charlie started shifting again. "Chief, there's been a lot of rumbling about the murders. People are asking us a lot of questions. We haven't said anything because we don't know anything." He exhaled, still shifting. "What I'm trying to say is we know you're taking a lot of heat. If there's anything we can do, extra I mean, just ask, okay?"

Charlie didn't know it, but he was a constant source of humor. After seven years of being under my command, he still had a problem talking to me in an official capacity. I liked him.

"I appreciate it, fellows. And if I *do* need help, you'll be the first to know."

They'd no sooner left the office when Marty walked in wearing a smile wider than usual.

"Sergeant Fee would like you to call her," she sang.

"Don't start with me, Marty."

"Moi? Would I do that?"

"And close the door on your way out."

She snapped to attention and saluted. "Yes sir."

I waited until she was gone to pick up the receiver. Before I'd punched in the first number, two sharp raps on the door preceded Charlie walking inside. When he saw me, he hesitated. I replaced the receiver.

"Sorry, Chief, but I was wondering if I could I talk to you? It's kind of personal."

"Sure, Charlie, just a second." I rose, closed the door, and returned to my chair.

Charlie began shifting again so I told him to sit down.

"Chief, first of all I have no problem with the swap. I understand why Reed wants to do it."

I shrugged. "Okay."

Charlie glanced down at my desk. "It's just that Reed's been acting kind of strange lately."

"How do you mean?"

"When he first started working here we used to eat together during the shift. Now he's not interested. He tells me he's already eaten or he's not hungry."

I sat back in my chair. "Well, no offense, Charlie, but maybe he's got other things on his mind."

"We used to get together after work. You know, for a beer. We don't do that anymore, either."

"I don't think he has anything against you. Now that he's been here a while, maybe he wants to meet with his other friends."

Charlie nodded, but I could tell there was more to it.

"Chief, he's been asking a lot of questions about Barney and Bo."

"What sort of questions?"

"Where they eat when they're on the night shift. Do they swap sectors often. Do they sleep on the job."

"I hope none of you sleeps on the job."

Charlie shook his head. "That's not what I mean. He

seems more interested in their routine than in what they're doing."

A cold feeling began to chill my insides. "What do *you* think?"

"At first I thought it was just Reed being Reed. But when he asked me if they'd noticed anything suspicious going on after Lucy Jarvis was murdered, I began to wonder."

I suddenly felt trapped. I didn't want to show all my cards, but I didn't want to lie to him, either.

"Charlie, you and I both know how eager Reed is to do well. I don't think his behavior is cause for alarm, but keep me posted, will you?"

Charlie lowered his head. "I feel like a rat, Chief."

"You're not a rat. I have to know what's going on out there. Keeping the lines of communication open with my men is the only way to do that."

Charlie looked up and offered a weak smile. "Thanks, Chief."

After he left the office, the chill inside me turned to solid ice. I really didn't want to believe that Reed had anything to do with the murder of Lucy Jarvis—or any murder for that matter.

I reached for the phone and called Stevie.

"Eldon, the fingerprints on the pendant don't belong to Seth Russell. Sandy's going to run a wider search."

"Oh."

"Yeah, I know how you feel. I was hoping we might have our first decent lead."

A thought wandered into my mind. "Say, Stevie, why were Russell's fingerprints in the system?"

"He used to work for Whitted Communications Incorporated, a company in Iowa that manufactures drone missile guidance systems for the military."

I remembered Iowa being one of Seth's stopping off points during his time in the Midwest. *At least he wasn't lying about that*, I thought.

"Oh, Eldon, before I forget, I spoke to Hannah McClatchy's supervisor yesterday. She said McClatchy was dating a guy she met a month ago, but she couldn't remember his name."

"Wouldn't it be something if it was Seth Russell?"

"I mentioned his name, but she didn't recognize it. However, she did say he was a salesman."

"Stevie, this is a shot in the dark, but would you mind checking to see if McClatchy's firm has any clients like Whitted Communications."

"Good idea, Eldon. I'll call you when I find out." Her voice softened. "And thanks again for a wonderful evening. I won't ever forget it."

I groaned. "Stevie, I'm beginning to think—"

Her laughter stopped me in mid-sentence.

"I'm sorry, Eldon. It's not often I get the opportunity to tease someone."

"You're starting to sound like my dispatcher."

"Oh? Does she enjoy giving you a good ribbing now and then?"

"*Too much* in my way of thinking."

"She must have a good sense of humor."

"I have that effect on younger women."

The day progressed without excitement and came to a close with no word from Stevie. I called her office, and when told she was out, left a message. Although I was still thinking about the recent developments, I promised myself that nothing was going to ruin my weekend.

• • EIGHTEEN • •

SATURDAY MORNING I WOKE UP with the sun, feeling better than I had in quite some time. After a shower and several cups of coffee, I decided it was time for breakfast.

Twenty minutes later a stack of waffles dripping with butter and maple syrup sat on a plate in front of me. Resisting the temptation to grab a fork and attack, I knew an important decision had to be made. Which of the four planks of bacon surrounding the stack should I devour first?

"You lose, pork boy," I said, and snatched up the strip nearest my right hand. I shoveled the entire plank into my mouth, but didn't get the chance to enjoy the waffles.

My cell phone put an end to the celebration.

"Eldon, I'm sorry to bother you so early on a Saturday."

"That's okay, Stevie. I wasn't doing anything important."

"Sandy and I got a call after I spoke to you yesterday.

It took up the rest of the day, and we didn't get back to the office until late last night."

"I figured as much."

"Sandy just finished the search. We found a match for the fingerprints. Look, there's no easy way to say this. The prints belong to one of your people, a Reed William Logan. Was he the officer who found it?"

"Logan! Are you sure?"

"A ten-point match."

"Another officer, Barney Andrews, found it, but he wouldn't..." Now the wheels were turning. "Stevie, did you find any prints at your crime scene?"

"Not a one. Eldon, I know what you're thinking, but we can't ignore it."

"Reed admitted to me that he drove by Hannigan's."

"You never told me that!"

"I didn't think it was necessary." My stomach tightened at the thought of Reed being involved. Stevie's silence compounded my anxiety. "I'll talk to him on Monday."

"I'm sorry, Eldon. I wish it could have been anyone else."

"Yeah, me, too."

"Just make sure you...you know."

"Make sure I what, Stevie?"

"I feel like I'm preaching to the choir. Just be careful, okay? You know what they say about desperate people."

Her genuine concern was swept away by a growing disgust inside me. I have no sympathy for dirty cops. Line them up against a wall is my philosophy. But of all people, why Reed? What prompted him to this course in life when he possessed everything necessary to write his own ticket? I began to seethe with prejudice. Doubt that Reed *might* be a victim of circumstance didn't enter my mind. No battle of conscience ensued, jaded on my part, convicting him before he offered a defense.

"Thanks for getting back to me, Stevie."

"I'm sorry, Eldon."

My stomach drew tighter as I pushed the plate away and sat back. *So much for my weekend*, I thought.

Throughout the day and into Sunday I worried about my next course of action. To brand Reed a perpetrator without hearing his side of the story was wrong. But I couldn't stand by and hope he was innocent, either. And something else was beginning to irritate me. Weeks ago, Marty mentioned a feeling that she was being followed. After my interactions with Seth, I automatically suspected him. Now I was wondering if a stalker *did* exist, was it Reed?

• • NINETEEN • •

MARTY SENSED TROUBLE the minute I walked into the office on Monday morning. Remaining reticent, she cut a sideward glance as I passed by, waiting for me to settle at my desk.

Moments later she appeared in the doorway wearing the look of a frightened child. She closed the door, walked to my desk, and set down a cup of coffee.

"What's wrong, Eldon?"

"Barney found a gold pendant where Mullen was murdered. I took it to the sheriff's office to be analyzed. They found Reed's fingerprints on it."

"Oh, no! What are you going to do?"

"I'm going to get to the bottom of it."

"But there's a chance he may not be guilty, right?"

Something about the way she said "guilty" sent a tremor through me.

"There's always a chance, but at this point I can't take anything for granted."

"He deserves the benefit of the doubt."

"I know, but I have to follow through on this."

Marty knew where I was heading. Some people are born to be successful. Reed was no exception. He exuded such professional confidence that one couldn't help but stand up and cheer. To think he would throw it all away for *any* reason was mind-boggling.

"Marty, I hope I'm wrong, but if I'm not…"

"I understand."

"This conversation stays between us."

She nodded.

"Marty, I need your input. You notice things about the way people dress and such, right? Ever notice Reed wearing jewelry? Other than his watch?"

"Not around here. I've only seen him once off the job. He wore a couple of rings but nothing else. Nothing I could see, anyway."

"Why would he have a gold pendant?"

"For a present, maybe? You know he's a player."

"Ever heard him speak of a woman named Nancy?"

"No. Why don't you ask Charlie."

"Care to help me figure out how to do that without sounding sneaky."

She offered a tight smile. "Good luck."

"I'm going for a ride. I don't know when I'll be back."

"I won't bother you unless it's important."

She knew me too well.

I took rides to think or check on things, and I disliked being interrupted. I headed straight to the Oyster Point docks to poke around. Life had returned to normal, and the destroyed portion of the pier had been rebuilt. No one seemed to miss Lucy Jarvis. The ground where she died lay bare. No flowers or memorial. Sad in a sense.

I walked the length of the seawall looking for anything, expecting nothing, and hoping for something. The dock workers and fishermen leveled odd stares, but true to their loathing of police, went about their business.

I mounted the dock and approached a deck hand on board the *Ophelia III*. The lean fisherman glanced in my direction as he worked on a winch motor. He wiped the sweat from his forehead with the back of his hand, and quickly looked away.

"Warmed up fast today, huh?" I said.

He looked up and ran a hand through his stringy black hair. His face was deeply tanned. His unfriendly brown eyes stared out through a permanent squint.

"Mind if I ask you a few questions?"

"Ain't gotta choice, do I?"

"I guess you know about Lucy Jarvis. Did she work on your boat?"

"Ain't my boat. And the captain ain't here."

"Which one did she work on?"

"None that I know. She was a cutter."

"Did she keep company with anyone in particular?"

"Couldn't tell you."

"You never saw her hanging around with any of the other guys?"

"Nope."

"She just came out here, did her job, and left?"

He shrugged. "Pretty much."

"Listen, what's your name?"

"Jimmy Summers."

"Jimmy, Lucy was one of you, and I'm trying to find her killer. Can you tell me *anything* about her?"

Jimmy looked toward Gulf Boulevard. "Can't help you."

I continued down the line of boats and received the same cold reception. No one wanted the others to know that he'd helped the police.

I knew beforehand that my attempt to find some answers would probably be a waste of time. I was hoping at least one fisherman would offer something useful. True to their unwritten code of silence, each man said little or nothing.

About the time I'd decided to leave, I noticed a fellow standing by a spigot mounted on a piling. As he washed his hands, he glanced at me several times looking uneasy. My gut told me to question him.

"You guys heading out any time soon?"

"I don't think so," he said. He cupped his hands, filled them with water, and splashed it into his blonde hair. "Too much work to do."

"Did you know Lucy Jarvis?"

"The cutter? Nah, not really." He looked away, his eyes darting up and down the line of boats.

"Ever see her talking to anyone? Other than you guys, I mean?"

"I didn't hardly see her at all."

Too many years of questioning suspects told me he wanted to say something, but knew better.

"What's your name?"

He peered over his shoulder at the boats again. "Davey Hooten."

"I'm Chief Eldon Quick, Davey. If you hear anything, give me a call, will you?"

He turned back, stared at my name plate then dropped his eyes to the spigot.

I left him for the parking lot and got into my SUV.

I arrived a few minutes later at the Happy Clam

motel, deciding to engage in a similar search of the area behind it.

I must have looked dazed and confused to the beach-goers in their swimsuits and sandals. Here I stood in full uniform, staring at the sand.

I conjured up an image of Reed and imagined him arm-in-arm with Nancy, his faceless date. Laughing and joking, maybe playing grab-ass, they paused by the spot where Mullen would die. Distracting her with the stars or maybe a kiss, he pulled the pendant from his pocket—a surprise not afforded the other women in his life. Nancy squealed with excitement or said nothing, her mouth agape. Reed smiled and clasped the pendant around her neck.

How did she lose it? I thought. *Did she lose it*?

Maybe Reed dropped it and was too embarrassed to say so. A small object lost in sugar sand at night could stay hidden forever.

"And maybe I'm wrong," I whispered. "Maybe Reed used the pendant as a bribe to bait Mullen."

"Who's that policeman talking to, Mommy?" a small voice behind me said.

I turned to discover a young woman with two children in tow. I smiled at the one little girl with a finger in her mouth.

"Grown-ups do that sometimes, honey," I said.

To hide my embarrassment, I quick-stepped back to my SUV knowing that even a child her age would think I was crazy. Frustration began to mount so I left the Happy Clam for Deemer's Inlet Park, the official monument to the town's reluctant founder, Wiley Deemer.

● ● ●

You'd think I'd be used to the mysterious appearances of Barney. Still, the sight of his patrol car got me to laughing—a sound absent for far too long. He was standing where the grass met the sand, looking out over the Gulf of Mexico. He didn't move when I strode up behind him.

"There's a lotta fish out there a-waitin' for us ta catch 'em, Chief."

"I know, Barney. One marlin in particular."

"We'd hafta go out quite a ways if ya want one that big."

"Do I have to ask how you knew I'd be here?"

He chuckled and looked down at his boots. "I called Marty. She said you was takin' a ride. You always come here ta think."

"Barney, when I retire, I'm going to recommend you for chief."

"Naw, not me. Too much horse hockey ta deal with."

"So to what do I owe the pleasure of your company?"

"I checked on them tattoo parlors. Ol' Mullet went ta one in Treasure Island. The guy there knows him, and said he'd been in before."

"And Lucy Jarvis?"

"Don't know fer positive about her. Some of the fellers I know on the boats said she mighta gone ta a place in Mad Beach. I talked to a feller there, but he said he didn't remember. I think he was lyin', though, 'cause he remembered the tattoo. Showed me a pitcher of it."

"How much did it cost?"

"The feller in T.I. said sevendee-five dollars."

"I can't see Mullen *or* Jarvis having that kind of money to throw around. Fishermen these days barely make enough to survive."

"I'm with you. I think Jarvis mighta worked out a trade fer hers. And I think they both was up ta somethin'."

I scanned the horizon and the storm clouds building in the distance. "You think they were involved with smuggling?"

"Maybe so. They's boats goin' in and outta here all the time. Course that means lots of others could be in on it, too."

"What do you *really* think?"

"You know, when ol' Deemer was fishin' these waters he found this place loaded with crabs. This spot right here. It didn't look like much from out there in the Gulf, so nobody paid it no mind. But he still worried 'bout them other fellers findin' it. After he laid his traps, he stuck a pole in the water. Right out yonder in the mouth. He put up a sign sayin' MINE! W.D. Them other trappers was so scared of him 'cause he was so mean, they didn't thinka tryin' ta poach his traps. Yep, word spread fast ta steer clear o' Deemer's Inlet." Barney chuckled. "And ya know, Chief, they got the name all wrong. They ain't no other inlets on this side o' Florida. They's all on the east side."

I let Barney go on because I knew he was eventually going to make a point.

"'Course they's talk that he once caught a feller poachin', and after he killed 'im, he split 'im wide open and used his guts fer bait."

Do you believe that story?"

Barney grinned. "Nope, but it shore is colorful. Anyway, if somebody was as mean as ol' Deemer, and felt like they was gettin' poached, they might just kill a coupla people ta scare hell out the others."

"So, Mullen and Jarvis were a message?"

"Them tattoos makes 'em part of somethin'. With them out the way, they'd be more money fer the rest."

"Barney, Mullen and Jarvis weren't the only ones killed."

"I know."

Of course you do, I thought.

"But the ring leader's gotta be somebody with lotsa brains."

I lowered my head.

"What's wrong, Chief?"

"Reed Logan may be involved."

"Naw, not Reed. I cain't believe that."

"His fingerprints were on the pendant."

Barney raised his eyebrows. "Do tell."

"Have you ever seen any tattoos on him?"

"Nope, but I know somebody who might."

"Do I want to know this person's name?"

"Best not ta sail them waters. At least not just yet."

"Get back to me as soon as you can. I'm going to confront him before he starts his shift."

Knowing about the tattoos would better my position when talking to Reed. His finger- prints on the pendant still bothered me, though.

· · TWENTY · ·

UNCERTAINTY STAYED WITH ME right up until my meeting with Reed Logan. While I don't care to be cornered, nor do I use the tactic on others, especially fellow officers, a tip off serves no purpose when searching for the truth. Reed was walking into an ambush. His defense and body language would weigh heavily in my determining his guilt or innocence.

A temporary distraction came when Stevie called to tell me that Hannah McClatchy's firm did, indeed, have two clients similar to Whitted Communications. Seth Russell's stock rose sharply, thrusting him into the spotlight as lead suspect.

I had to address the matter closer to home first.

When Reed walked into my office, his ignorance of the impending interrogation was obvious. He only became concerned when he looked over his shoulder and saw Barney enter and close the door.

"What's this all about?"

"I have a problem and I need your help," I said. I

glanced at Barney. He shook his head, indicating that no tattoo existed.

"Certainly, Chief, whatever I can do."

"We recently found a gold pendant near the site where Mullet Mullen was killed."

Reed remained silent.

"Know anything about it?"

"Should I?"

"That's what I'm asking you."

"I don't recall knowing of, or owning a pendant."

Nicely worded, I thought. "Then here's my problem. We found your fingerprints on it."

Reed didn't flinch, shift, or change expression. "I don't see how that's possible. I've never owned anything like—" His eyes widened slightly. "Check that, Chief, I forgot. I did buy a pendant as a gift."

"Mind telling me how it wound up behind the Happy Clam?"

"My girlfriend and I were there one night. A few days before the murder."

"How did she lose it?"

"She didn't, I did. I dropped it in the sand before I had a chance to give it to her. She didn't notice so I didn't say anything."

"What's your girlfriend's name?"

"Nancy Wisnewsky."

"And she can corroborate your story?"

"About being there? Yes. About the pendant? No."

"Why didn't you mention this when we found Mullen?"

"With all due respect, I just said I forgot."

Convenient, I thought. "Okay, Reed, I'm satisfied. And I hope you understand the purpose of this meeting."

"Yes, sir, I fully understand. But for the record, I'm offended that anyone would believe me party to *any* criminal activity."

"So noted."

He left without acknowledging either of us. Barney took a seat in front of my desk.

"What do you think?" I asked.

"Well, he didn't act nervous or stutter or nothin'. He's pretty dang cool 'bout the whole thing."

"A little too cool in my book."

Barney grinned. "Ol' Reed's a smart feller. I gotta feelin' he's been a-sittin' on the griddle before."

"That's what I mean. Thinking on your feet is one thing. His answers sounded rehearsed like he knew the questions in advance."

Barney paused a moment, thinking. "I s'pose so. If he was up ta somethin', though, he'd have ta be ready in case he got caught. You gonna call his girlfriend?"

"That's another thing. He admitted seeing me at Hannigan's while on a date *with* Nancy Wisnewsky."

"I ain't followin' ya, Chief."

"In the course of conversation, I asked him if she was special. He said no. You just heard him call her his girlfriend. And he was giving her a gift *before* all this happened."

"Chief, I ain't sayin' you're wrong, but everybody knows he likes the ladies. Maybe he didn't want ta ruin his reputation."

"That could be, but—"

"I know, until this thing is settled, you cain't let nothin' slide."

"Thanks for your help, Barney."

Later that afternoon I called the office of Nancy Wisnewsky at the Bayboro Campus of the University of South Florida. Her administrative assistant informed me that *Doctor* Wisnewsky was still with her students doing field research somewhere on Tampa Bay. She was due back in a couple of hours. Discovering her to be a marine biologist somewhat lessened my slant on Reed.

At least he has good taste, I thought.

At the same time a menacing ache in my stomach refused to go away. Like Seth, Reed possessed a persuasive quality—an ability to lead people in the direction of his choosing. I'd witnessed firsthand his defusing of a volatile situation during a potential bar fight.

Stepping between the drunken pair, his commanding demeanor and cool-headedness resulted in both parties returning to their tables, each respecting the intervention and happy not to be going to jail.

Had Reed seduced Nancy Wisnewsky into becoming a willing ally? Or did she unknowingly provide the alibi to cover his tracks? Maybe she'd been the bait to lure Mullen to his death. I wouldn't know until I spoke with her. And even then, would I *really* know? I called an end to my session of personal brow-beating a half hour later.

"Marty, I'm going for a ride and then I'm going home."

Marty glanced at her watch. "Okay, I'll…okay."

"Is something wrong?"

"I was just going to ask you if I could leave early. I have some things I need to do."

"No problem. I'll see you tomorrow."

"Thanks, Eldon. I meant to say something earlier."

Marty *never* had a problem making such requests. Her fidgeting told me that whatever the reason, she was on edge.

I headed to the Bayboro campus on the off chance that Nancy Wisnewsky had returned from her field trip. I hadn't been in downtown St Petersburg for quite some time. The changes were a mild surprise. All for the better I might add.

I found the university parking lot on Sixth Avenue South, and made my way to the Biological Sciences building. Told that she had recently returned, I realized my wait for the unannounced visit would be brief.

Doctor Nancy Wisnewsky was a cheerful, auburn-haired woman with an engaging smile and a figure that would be the envy of most college girls. I could understand the ease in which a man might become attracted to her.

After explaining my reason for being there, we went to her office and to converse.

"I appreciate your seeing me, Doctor. I'm sure your schedule is full."

"You caught me at the right time, Chief Quick. I just returned from the field. Please excuse my t-shirt and blue jeans."

A most likable person, I thought. "Doctor, I have some questions for you."

"May I ask what this is about?"

"I understand you've been dating one of my officers. Reed Logan."

"Oh, yes, for quite some time now. He speaks highly of you."

"Doctor, this next question may sound strange, but has he ever given you any gifts?"

Wisnewsky chuckled. "Yes, and I wish he'd stop. I think he's getting serious."

I narrowed my eyes. "Is there a problem?"

"No, no, I'm just old fashioned. I don't like to rush into things." She tilted her head. "Reed's not in trouble, is he?"

"Would you mind telling me what he's given you?"

Wisnewsky brought her right index finger to her face and tapped her chin. "Let's see, besides flowers, he's big on flowers, he's given me a watch and a necklace."

"Anything else?"

"No, but there *was* one time…"

"What do you mean?"

"We'd taken a walk on the beach one night. In Deemer's Inlet as a matter of fact. We were going back to the car when Reed stopped and started talking about personal things. I knew he was up to something. He's pulled that routine on me before. Anyway, he pointed at the stars and I looked up. When nothing happened, I turned back to him. He had this strange look on his face. Like he was uncomfortable with something that had happened. He never said anything, and I didn't make an issue of it. I didn't want to embarrass him."

"Do you remember when you were there?"

"About a month or two ago. Maybe less. I don't remember the day."

"Thank you for your time, Doctor."

Wisnewsky leaned forward in her chair. Concern was shaping her face. "Chief Quick, I hope I haven't gotten Reed into trouble. I really like him."

I smiled. "Not to worry, Doctor."

My mood was a little better when I left the parking lot, but I still wasn't convinced of Reed's innocence.

• • TWENTY-ONE • •

I CRACKED OPEN A BEER and immediately retired to my lawn chair. Beaten down by the day, I needed to relax. The uncertainty surrounding the meeting with Reed stayed burrowed in my mind, rejecting the liquid anesthesia I poured into my body. A second beer helped draw my attention to the attractiveness of the Intracoastal Waterway. A seagull swooped low, graceful, and skimmed the surface before soaring upwards. The cicadas were in full voice and sang in perfect harmony. Beautiful. A reminder of the reason I moved here.

Swinging my feet to the patio deck, I raised my right arm, flipped my wrist, and let the empty beer can roll off my fingertips. The can spun end over end and found the tan plastic trash basket for a perfect two-pointer.

"Nothing but bag!" I shouted and stood up, imitating a cheering crowd. In the middle of my victory salsa dance, I heard someone knock on the front door. I continued to celebrate and danced into the house.

"Stevie, what a surprise."

"I'm sorry I didn't call first, Eldon."

"Well don't just stand there, come on in."

Stevie dropped her head. "I was on my way home and couldn't stop thinking about the murders. Eldon, I hate to jump you like this, but I need to run something by you."

"Sure, we'll sit on the patio. I was about to get a beer. I don't have any—"

"I'd love one, thanks."

I grabbed two beers, opened them, and slid a big bag of pretzels under my arm. I remembered her partner Sandy Baker's warning about Stevie and her moods. As I joined her on the patio, I sat down, handed her a beer, and fastened my seat belt.

After a long gulp, Stevie dove right in. "Now suppose, just *suppose*, they're all in on it. All of them."

"All of them," I said. "You mean Russell, McClatchy, Mullen, Jarvis, and—"

"Yes. McClatchy has access to the clients. She contacts Russell. He wins them over, and through them scams extra products for private sales."

"Products?"

"Products like, oh, I don't know, something that could turn a huge profit. Drugs or guns maybe."

"He told me he's currently hawking automotive and industrial batteries."

"Okay. Maybe not drugs or guns." Stevie took another swig. "There has to be a common denominator for them taking such a big risk."

I thought a moment. "We know that Russell worked for that company in Iowa. What was the name?"

"Whitted Communications Incorporated."

"And they make parts for missile guidance systems.

I wonder if—"

"Industrial batteries!" Stevie nearly spilled her beer.

"What?"

"Industrial batteries! Don't you see? Industrial batteries or *any* product that can be used for defense systems."

"But how do you know he—"

"I checked on him. Every company he's worked for has manufactured a product that directly or indirectly can be of use."

"And he sells them on the black market?"

"That's got to be it."

"So he must have a specific clientele."

"Not necessarily. We don't know how long he's been at this, or how he got started. Maybe the interested parties contact him, and the highest bidder wins out."

"Okay, I'm with you so far."

"Transporting is the next question, though. Russell would have to involve some people in shipping to make certain no questions were asked. That could be tricky when he's bouncing from one company to another."

"Not if the parts are travelling with a legitimate sale." Another question rolled into my head. "I wonder how they would be separated at the destination point."

Stevie took another gulp of beer, her eyes flitting from side to side. "Wait a minute! Who in shipping questions where the products are going? Box up the order, slap a label on it, and be done. And what semi driver cares if he delivers it to a dock or a warehouse?"

"Good point, Stevie. In fact, it's a *very* good point. But in this case, why wouldn't

Russell keep his dealings in Tampa where he says his clients are located?"

"Scrutiny. *Everything* can't be shipped out of the Port of Tampa all of the time. Someone would catch on."

I nodded. "So he fans out to smaller ports for the smaller cargo, keeping a low profile."

"Exactly. And sometimes he uses fishing boats. It's a perfect cover."

I still wasn't convinced. "So how does Jbara, the accountant, fit into this group? He worked in Clearwater."

Stevie didn't blink. "But he *moved* from Tampa. And guess who contracted his firm on occasion?"

"McClatchy's employer, Leventhal and Rand."

"You need an accountant to cook the books. Maybe he was the one keeping it legal on paper."

"So why was Jbara killed?"

"Maybe he got greedy or wanted out. His behavior became the catalyst for killing the others."

"I don't know, Stevie. That's quite a stretch. It's all quite a stretch."

Stevie lowered her eyes. A moment later she looked up. "I've considered another possibility. What if Russell eliminates his partners before he bails?"

"That would be a smart move on his part, but he's only been here two months."

"What if Jbara became the weak link. Maybe Russell feared a domino effect, that all of them might cave in."

I shook my head. "Stevie, there almost certainly are more players involved than we
know."

"Aren't there always?"

"Killing all of his co-conspirators would be too risky, not to mention the time involved."

Stevie paused to study the beer in her grasp.

"So tell me. How does my deputy fit into all this?"

Stevie looked up with her face pinched into a grimace. "Security. He knows the schedule and the monthly shift changes, right? Most patrolmen are creatures of habit. He would know who was where and when. I know they change their patrol routes to offset boredom, but even if he was checking on them while off duty he would have a good idea. What's wrong, Eldon?"

Deceit drove a dagger into my heart. To think that by design Reed would run interference for Russell's operation cut me to the core.

"Nothing. What you're saying makes sense."

Our conversation lasted another four hours until, exhausted, we agreed to call it a night.

I didn't go to sleep right way. I went to bed, but tossed and turned thinking Stevie's theory might be right. Such widespread undertakings are far above my level of understanding. Greater minds had no problem conceiving them. And Barney's words kept echoing.

"The ring leader's gotta be somebody with lotsa brains."

Sleep overcame me without permission, not that I minded.

A sound I'd come to despise yanked me from serenity. My cell phone is heartless.

"Charlie's been shot!" Reed cried.

"What! When?"

"I just got here. They're working on him now. I was all the way on the south end. I got here as fast as I could."

"Reed, where are you?"

"I'm at the park. At Deemer's Inlet Park."

"I'll be right there!"

I jumped out of bed, got dressed, and dashed to my SUV. The sound of spinning tires and the smell of burning rubber split the night air as I raced down the street, making a hard-right turn onto Sand Dollar Drive. I hit the red and blue warning lights, ignored the stop sign at Gulf Boulevard, and made another hard right.

Deemer's Inlet Park was five minutes from my home, a short distance made longer by the flashbacks streaming into my mind. The same grip of helplessness I'd felt when my partner in Miami went down contorted my insides—a twisting and nauseating sensation.

In the distance I saw an ambulance enter Gulf Boulevard and head north with its red lights igniting the darkness and its mournful siren wailing. After a sharp left into the parking lot, I leapt from my vehicle and hurried to a small group huddled by the entrance.

Two Indian Rocks Beach patrolmen and a Sheriff's deputy stood beside Reed. Their faces verified my worst fear. Reed was hunched over, his face drawn and close to tears.

"How's Charlie? Is he okay?" I said in a low voice.

The deputy faced me. "It looked bad, but I don't know. The EMTs wouldn't say."

I placed a hand on Reed's shoulder. "Tell me what happened."

"I don't know. He called me on the radio. Right after he got shot." He choked on the words and swallowed hard. "I couldn't get here in time. I tried, but I was too far…" He broke down and began to cry.

One of the Indian Rocks Beach patrolmen motioned with his head. He and I moved a few steps away.

"Officer Grayson, Chief. I was first on the scene. I

had just turned around at the city limits when I heard the call." He took a breath. "When I got here, Charlie was over there where you see the cones. I notified Dispatch then I called Crime Scene."

"You know Charlie?"

He nodded, taking another breath. "No one was here. Just Charlie." He gestured to a pair of bystanders. "Those two were fishing on the beach. They said didn't see anyone."

"Thanks for getting here so fast."

"Chief, Charlie wasn't one to let his guard down. He took two rounds right above the neckline of his vest. Whoever did this must have surprised him. They knew right where to aim."

"Probably some punk high on something," I grumbled.

Grayson looked toward the cones. "I don't know, Chief. I looked around after the ambulance got here, but I didn't find anything. Kind of hard with just a flashlight. I doubt if they'll find any footprints. Nothin' but sidewalk and asphalt and grass around here." He ran a hand across his forehead.

I thanked the patrolman again and went back to Reed.

"Why don't you go home. You're in no condition to work."

Reed looked up, his face drenched in tears. "But what about my—"

"I'll make sure we're covered. Now, go home. That's an order."

He trudged back to his patrol car with his head bowed low.

I'd been there before. Thousands of times I'd re-lived

the shooting of my partner. Wishing I'd reacted sooner. Wishing it was me.

While waiting for the Crime Scene Unit, I decided I'd better call in Barney.

He agreed to cover Reed's shift, and thirty minutes later, arrived with a thermos of hot coffee.

"Here," he said as he handed me a cup, "Sue Ellen thought ya might need this."

"Sue Ellen's a fine woman, Barney."

"Heard anythin' 'bout Charlie?"

"No. I guess I should call the hospital."

Barney looked down at his cup. "Do ya think Reed knew 'bout this?"

"If he did, he's a good actor. He was all torn up. He blames himself."

"Nothin' he coulda' done, I s'pose. If he *didn't* know, I mean."

"He said he was on the south end when Charlie called him."

"Charlie called him?"

"Right after he was shot."

Barney swirled his coffee and drank it.

"If something's on your mind, speak up."

"How long ya figure it takes ta get here from the south end?"

"This time of night? Two, maybe three minutes."

"Uh-huh."

"Spit it out, Barney. I'm too tired to do this."

"Now I'm just sayin', but if it was me, wouldn't hell nor high water keep me from gettin' here."

I took a few seconds to consider what he'd said. "Have you mentioned this to anyone else?"

"Nope."

I glanced around to make sure no one was standing nearby. "Charlie and Reed talked to me about swapping sectors. Now this happens. Does that seem odd to you?"

"I don't know, Chief. Bo and me swap all the time. Maybe it was just bad luck."

"But you just said—"

"I know, but, well, maybe Reed couldn't believe it at first. Maybe he was stunned."

"Has any other officer been shot since you started working here?"

"Nope. Chief Bevins was proud of that, too. He said we was real lucky."

Lucky is right, I thought.

I left Barney to go give Charlie's wife, Cindy, the bad news. Leaving Barney alone without backup under *any* circumstance was not a good idea, but Cindy needed to be notified. A part of my job I really hated, but had to be done.

The deputy and two patrolmen offered to help so I accepted. I called Bo Simpson anyway. Like Barney, Bo immediately agreed to come in, though I could tell the reason shook him up. He and Barney worked well together. I felt a degree of relief as I left.

When Cindy Bates opened the front door she smiled initially, even half asleep, then her face became contorted with worry. I told her what happened, and she fought to restrain her emotions. I waited while she got dressed, and walked her to my SUV.

When we arrived at the hospital, we were told that Charlie was still in surgery. His condition was critical.

I sat down with Cindy and held her hand, unable to find the right words.

Cindy dabbed her eyes with a Kleenex. "I knew this day would come," she said. "I always had a feeling that one day this would happen."

"Cindy, don't do this to yourself. We can never know about these things. Charlie's tough, and he's going to make it."

Cindy nodded and tried to smile. She wanted to believe me.

Charlie died on the operating table ten minutes later. The doctor said the damage was too extensive, and he'd lost too much blood.

I drove Cindy home to make sure she got there safely, and I stayed with her until her sister and brother-in-law arrived.

• • TWENTY-TWO • •

THE SUN WAS SITTING a shade above the horizon when I started back to the station. It was the longest trip of my life.

I'd been in a daze when my partner was shot, and wracked with pain when my wife passed away. Losing Charlie felt like a part of me died with him.

When I entered the office, I discovered Marty at her desk, her eyes red and swollen.

"I just can't believe it," she said and sniffed. "Charlie didn't deserve to die like that."

"Marty, why don't you go home. You're in no condition to—"

"No! I want to stay. You're short-handed as it is, and I…I don't want to be alone." She covered her face with both hands and began to cry.

Barney and Bo walked in, saw Marty, and lowered their heads.

"Chief, Bo and me would like ta talk ta you," Barney said in a low voice.

"Sure."

I squeezed Marty's shoulder before the three of us went into my office.

"Considerin' our situation, Bo and me will do what needs ta be done," Barney said.

"Yeah, Chief. I called Annie and we talked it over," Bo said. "I'll hold off on my vacation until we get things squared away."

"I appreciate it, fellows, but I'm going to call Indian Rocks Beach and borrow a couple of their men for the time being. Bo, take your vacation. Annie deserves some time away from here. And so do you. We'll manage until you get back."

I heard the outer door close, and Marty say, "Reed, what are you doing here?"

I looked toward the doorway as Barney and Bo turned around. Reed walked in looking frail and tentative. Not the confident young buck he usually appeared.

"I had to come in, Chief." He coughed. "I had to."

I stared hard at him. "Are you sure you're up to it?"

"Yes, sir, I'm...yes, sir."

"Okay, take the south end. Bo, you take the north."

They left without further discussion.

I shifted my attention to Barney. "I hate to do this, but until I make arrangements with Indian Rocks, you and I will work nights. Tell Sue Ellen I'm sorry."

Barney gave me a tight grin. "Send 'er some flowers and take us out ta dinner when all this calms down. That'll make her happy."

"Deal."

Barney lost his grin as he closed the door. "Chief, I cain't stop thinking 'bout last night."

"I can't, either."

"I mean 'bout Reed."

"What's bothering you?"

Barney sat down and folded his arms. "You said he told you that Charlie called 'im after he got shot, right?"

"That's right."

"That Indian Rocks Beach feller said he got there first, and nobody was there 'cept Charlie, right?"

I nodded.

"Well, if it took Reed three minutes ta get ta the park, and he called you on the way, why didn't he get there first?"

"Grayson said he was at the city limits, a minute from the park."

Barney offered a blank stare. "Then shouldn't they've gotten there 'bout the same time?"

"Good point. I never asked Grayson when Reed arrived."

Barney scratched his head. "And somethin' else I don't get. I ain't no crime scene genius, but they was a awful lotta blood on the ground."

"Are you saying that Reed waited before responding?"

"I'm thinkin' more like it weren't Charlie who called 'im."

"The shooter? Barney, that doesn't make sense. If I shoot someone, I wouldn't tell anybody. Not right away, anyhow. Maybe never."

"*You* wouldn't. Most people wouldn't, I s'pect. But remember when we's talkin' about ol' Mullet and Lucy Jarvis gettin' killed might be some kinda message? Maybe Charlie gettin' killed was a message ta Reed."

Barney's claim took the wind right out of me. I pictured Seth calling Reed after he'd killed Charlie, boasting and threatening. My thoughts were interrupted by a peculiar look on Barney's face. He wasn't one to express his personal feelings, but he was easy to read if you were around him long enough.

"What're you thinking?"

Barney shifted in his chair. "I's just thinkin' 'bout Charlie." He looked down and fixed his eyes on the corner of my desk. "He's the one I asked 'bout Reed havin' a tattoo."

"How would he know?"

"Reed ran a coupla them marathons. You know, a bunch of guys in undershirts and shorts all tryin' ta get ta somewhere before the other. Charlie said Reed didn't even have a scar on him."

No tattoo and a solid alibi, I thought. "I talked to Reed's girlfriend."

"What'd she have ta say?"

"She verified Reed's story about the pendant. They were behind the Happy Clam. She thought he was going to give her a gift, but he didn't. What he said about dropping it was true, I guess."

"Or she's a good liar."

"So now you believe Reed *is* involved?"

"Hate ta say it, but I think ol' Reed's in way over his head and fixin' ta drown."

I paused and gave much thought to what I was about to say. I leaned forward and lowered my voice. "Over the past few weeks, I've found out a lot about Marty's boyfriend. I think he's the one behind this whole mess."

"Seth Russell?"

Of course you know his name, I thought.

"What're you gonna do?"

"I don't know yet. We've got no reason to arrest him. We could call him in for questioning, but he won't tell us anything. For all I know, he's already gone."

"You think he killed Charlie?"

"My money's on him."

"Then let's bring 'im in, anyway."

"We can try. I'll call the sheriff's office and have them go to his apartment."

"What 'bout Marty?"

"She and Seth have put their relationship on hold. And from what she tells me, I'm not so sure they'll get back together."

"Prob'ly for the best."

Again, we were interrupted.

"Eldon, the media's lined up in the parking lot," Marty said.

"I'll be right there."

"Well, I'm gettin' out of here. See you tonight, Chief."

I called Stevie and made arrangements for deputies to go to Seth's apartment. Questioning him about being at Hannigan's the night of Hannah McClatchy's murder seemed valid now. Stevie said she'd go with them.

The media blitz, and fielding calls from Sam Hackney and a number of others took up a good deal of the day.

Most of the calls were from the community offering their condolences. Quite a few came from the surrounding agencies, saddened by the loss of a brother-in-arms.

By two o'clock I was totally spent.

"Marty, I'm heading home to get some sleep."

"Did you call Indian Rocks Beach about borrowing some of their men?"

I froze in my tracks.

"Don't worry. I'll take care of it."

"What would I do without you?"

"Flattery will get you nowhere."

Never did, I thought.

"Eldon, I'll take the necessary paperwork to Cindy Bates. It's never a good time, but she needs to take care of it before the other stuff overwhelms her. And it'll give me a chance to check on her."

"Marty, I can do that tomorrow. You don't have to—"

"I want to. Now go! A man your age needs—"

"I know, I know," I said and waved her off.

I went home, cracked open a beer, and stretched out on my lawn chair. I should have gone straight to bed. In a few hours I'd be covering the night shift for Bo. I really needed to rest.

Charlie's death hit me hard, and though I tried to remain tough, I knew if I closed my eyes his image would find its way into my dreams. My chest began to tighten. I could feel the tears welling up. I took a pull of beer, and stared at the cobalt sky sitting atop the horizon. The sound of my cell phone reversed my feelings in an instant.

"Son-of-a-bitch!"

I pulled the menace from my pocket and answered.

"Eldon, it's Marty. I'm sorry to bother you, but I just got the strangest phone call."

"These days nothing surprises me."

"Some guy named Davey said he needs to talk to you right away."

I sat up straight and set my beer on the patio deck. "Did he say what he wanted?"

"No, just that he was waiting at a pay phone."

Marty passed along the number, and I thanked her. My body filled with anxiety as I punched in the number and waited. Davey was about to break the fisherman's code of silence, and I was eager to know why.

I heard him pick up the receiver, but he didn't answer.

"Davey, its Chief Quick."

"Listen up, Chief, 'cause I ain't got much time. Lucy Jarvis and the captain and crew of the *Orion* was up to somethin'. I dunno what."

"How do you know?"

"They went out a bunch of times. Always late at night. And they never brung in a haul. I heard some of the guys jawin' about it."

"So they had bad luck, so what?"

"Nobody ever knowed when they was goin' out. And none of them never said nothin' when they got back to port."

"Was anyone other than the captain and crew involved?"

"Yeah, Mullet Mullen. Before somebody did him."

"I thought Mullen worked in Madeira Beach?"

"He did. He's been run off of ever boat around here, but he started workin' the *Orion* again. Look, Chief, I got to go!"

"Davey, wait! Has anyone else been poking around Oyster Point? Someone you don't normally see, I mean."

The silence that followed told me my hunch was right.

"Yeah, a cop."

I knew Davey was scared by the way he slammed down the receiver. My mind began to race with a slew of possibilities. Only one name stood out—Reed Logan.

I picked up my beer and lay back in the chair.

· · TWENTY-THREE · ·

"PEG, ANSWER THE PHONE, will you? Peg? Peg!"

I jumped awake, and realized I'd been asleep.

The night creatures along the channel were chattering, and the cars moved with frequency along Gulf Boulevard as I pulled my cell phone from my pocket.

"Chief?"

"Barney! Aw, jeez, I overslept."

He laughed. "Chief, I never thought I'd hear muhself say this, but yer late fer work."

"I'll be right there!"

"Don't bother. I'm already patrolin' the south end. The north end's closer fer ya, anyhow."

Since I was still in uniform, I brushed my teeth, darted out the door, and was cruising the north end ten minutes later.

Good old Barney, I thought. *I owe him and Sue Ellen more than just one dinner out.*

I reached the town limits, doubled back, and pulled behind a strip mall. Shutting down my SUV, I brought out my cell phone to call Stevie.

"Eldon, you sound terrible. Are you feeling all right?"

"No, I'm not. Did you have any luck with Russell?"

"Sandy and I got a call right after I talked to you. The deputies went to his apartment, but he wasn't there. They didn't have a search warrant, so they couldn't go inside. They waited an hour but he didn't show. They went back later, but he still wasn't there."

"He's in the wind."

"I've got that feeling, too."

"I guess we can get his personal information from the apartment manager and try to track him down. If it's not bogus."

"I'll put out a state-wide alert. We'll find him. What are you doing now?"

"I'm on patrol."

"On patrol? Why are you…Oh, right, I heard about what happened. Sorry."

"We're getting a couple of men from Indian Rocks Beach tomorrow until we get back to full strength."

"You'll let me know if there's anything my office can do?"

"Sure will, and thanks, Stevie."

I was grateful the rest of the night remained quiet— quiet in the sense of no drunks or accidents.

Around midnight, Barney and I broke for dinner. Meeting halfway at Birnbaum's Restaurant, we reopened our conversation about Reed Logan.

Theory upon theory poured out of Barney concerning Reed's hand in Seth Russell's supposed operation. I made him aware of everything I knew, including

Stevie's findings and Davey Hooten's call.

"Chief, you sure the guy you talked to was Davey Hooten?" Barney asked.

"Young guy, blonde hair, brown eyes, lean and kind of mean looking."

"Yep, that's Davey." Barney looked down at his empty plate. "Don't know if I'd believe haffa what he said, though."

"But, Barney, why would he bother to call me?"

"Good point. He could be jackin' ya around, though. Ya know how them guys are. Course, either way he'd be takin' a big risk just talkin' ta you."

"For argument's sake, let's say only part of what he said is true."

"The question is which part? Usually haffa what Davey says is a lie, and the other haff is made up."

I was hoping Barney could offer a little more insight. He seemed to be as baffled as me.

"I don't really want to believe that a cop is involved."

Barney produced a tight smile. "You don't wanna believe that *Reed* is involved."

"No, I don't. So if it's just Jarvis, Mullen, and the Orion crew, then I'm still betting that Seth Russell is calling the shots."

Barney nodded. "I'd back ya on that."

I searched his eyes. "What do you *really* think?"

He ran a hand over the back of his neck. "I think they's all in on it."

I could hear Stevie's words again.

"Chief, I hate ta say it, but fer once in his life ol' Davey just might be tellin' the truth. And if that's the case then yer gonna hafta—"

"I know."

We agreed to corner Reed the next morning when we returned to the office, and pressure him into telling all he knew. If he didn't, well, evidence or not, I was going to arrest him.

At 2:23 a.m., I was trolling a side street, Abalone Avenue, and thinking about Charlie. Made quiet by the time of morning, the north end was still, oblivious to the one or two cars on the road and the insomniacs milling about inside their homes.

With all that had transpired I was still in somewhat of a daze. My cell phone rang and startled me. I almost hit a mailbox.

"Chief Quick, this is Officer Grayson, Indian Rocks Beach P.D."

"Officer Grayson, what's keeping you up so late?"

"Chief, we found a body on the beach at Starfish Park, shot twice in the throat. He has no identification on him, but we found your office number on a piece of paper in his pocket. Any idea of who he might be."

An icy surge of adrenaline shot through me. "Is he a skinny kid with blonde hair and brown eyes? Kind of rough looking?"

"Yes, sir."

"His name is Davey Hooten. He works on one of the boats at the Oyster Point docks."

"I wonder what he was doing up this way?"

"I have no idea, Officer."

"Chief, I have no right to ask you, but could this have something to do with Charlie? The bullet wounds look the same."

Since I didn't know the man I hesitated, and

wondered if he could be trusted. "It might, but I'd appreciate your keeping this under your hat for now. I'll call Chief Siddons in the morning."

"Yes, sir. And if there's anything I can do, just give me a call."

Davey Hooten's death sent me into a downward spiral. Someone connected to this whole mess found out about him. I wanted to nab that someone.

I wasn't a half-block from Gulf Boulevard on Manatee Way when my cell phone rang again. The name that appeared on the caller ID surprised me.

"Hi, Eldon, are you busy?" Marty said.

"Busy? At this time of the morning?"

"I couldn't sleep so I thought I'd..." She released a small squeak like she'd been poked in the ribs. "I need to talk to you, Eldon."

"Talk away. I'm just cruising."

"No, I mean in person."

Something about her voice sounded different. Marty spoke with a noticeable rhythm—inflections woven around her words. This voice carried a veil of ambiguity. Hesitancy draped over reluctance.

"You want to meet me somewhere? I'm on the north end."

"How about the park?"

"The park?"

"You know I don't like crowds."

"Okay, I'll be there in a few minutes."

Two things were bothering me as I turned onto Gulf Boulevard. I couldn't imagine Marty wanting to meet at the park in the middle of the night. Not after what happened. And Marty *loved* large events. A few people in a coffee shop wouldn't rattle her one bit.

•• TWENTY-FOUR ••

THE PARKING LOT WAS DESERTED and the grounds quiet as I chose a space close to the sidewalk. I quickly scanned the area, discovering a few shadows and a good many bugs flailing themselves against the light on the side of the restrooms. Sliding from my SUV, I quietly closed the door, crossed the sidewalk, and strode into the grass.

Two silhouettes stood facing the dark water on the white ring of sand. As I drew nearer, I pulled my Smith and Wesson .38 from its holster.

Less than fifteen feet separated us when the pair spun around. Light from a full moon shone down on the couple as I raised my pistol to shoulder level.

"Hi, Gramps. Long time, no see," Seth said.

His left arm clamped around Marty's throat forced her to act as a shield. The .380 automatic pressed into her neck was a persuasive inducement.

"Drop the gun, Seth!"

"Not going to happen, Gramps. I think you'd better

drop yours." He pressed the gun harder into Marty's neck.

"Don't be a fool. You're not getting out of here."

I had a clear shot to nail him in the head, but I noticed Marty's eyes had widened. She began to tremble.

Seth laughed low and vicious. "There's only one fool here, and I'm looking at him.

Even with a lucky shot, I'll still take her out. Do you want to risk it, old man? Huh? Do you?"

I wasn't about to surrender my weapon. "Let her go. Then I'll drop my gun."

Seth laughed again. "Oh, Gramps, you are *so* gallant and *so* brave. And you must think I'm stupid! Now drop your gun!"

"Or what, you'll kill her? You kill her, I kill you, and it's over. Is that the *real* reason for this get-together? Suicide by cop? Well, let's make it easy. You let her go, and I'll blow you away and everyone gets what they want."

"You're starting to piss me off, old man! You don't think I have the balls, do you?

"It doesn't take balls to kill an unarmed woman."

Marty screamed as Seth threw her aside and fired a split-second before I did. A third shot joined the cracking sound echoing through the line of Australian pines.

The pain I felt was indescribable. I grabbed my stomach and crumbled to the ground.

"Eldon!" Marty screamed, and dashed to my side. "Oh my god! Hold on, Eldon, hold on!" Marty started to reach for the radio microphone attached to my shirt.

Through blurry eyes I saw a figure walk up behind her. The figure leaned down and placed a hand on her shoulder.

"Are you all right, Chief?"

Marty jerked her head around. "Reed!"

I sat up slowly, grimacing with pain. "Feels like I got punched in the gut." I looked beyond them and saw Seth lying face down by the water's edge. I noticed my gun lying nearby, and picked it up as Marty and Reed helped me to my feet.

"I guess that vest did its job, huh, Chief?"

"Oh, Eldon." Marty threw her arms around me and buried her head in my chest. "Seth called me while I was with Cindy Bates. He said he wanted to talk. I didn't know what he was going to do. Oh, Eldon, I am *so* sorry."

I was thankful Reed appeared when he did. I hadn't seen him sneaking through the darkness and coming up behind Seth and Marty along the beach. But something else was bothering me besides my stomach.

I eased Marty away, and leveled my Smith and Wesson. "Give me your gun, Reed."

"Eldon, what are you doing? Reed just saved your life."

"Your gun."

Reed began to back up, his Beretta M9 hanging at arm's length. "I'm not a part of this, Chief. I didn't do anything wrong."

"You killed Charlie Bates."

Marty was stunned. "What! Reed killed Charlie? What are you talking about?"

"I didn't kill him! Russell did!"

"Russell ordered you to kill Charlie because you were in his pocket. You had to do it because Charlie found out, didn't he?"

"You've got it all wrong, Chief! Charlie called me

after he was shot!"

"I checked with the doctor. He told me there was no way Charlie could have called you. The location of his wound would have prevented him from talking. You knew *exactly* where to shoot him."

Reed stopped moving. "Chief, you're wrong!"

"Russell wanted me dead, too, but you couldn't do it. That's when he decided to grab Marty and lure me out here. You knew, didn't you, Reed? That's how you knew where to find us."

Panic covered Reed's face as he jerked up the Beretta.

A final shot rang out through the park.

• • TWENTY-FIVE • •

FOUR DAYS LATER I LAY stretched out on my lawn chair, cold beer in hand, and still hurting from the fist-sized bruise darkening my stomach. The clouds in the western sky were lining up to co-star with a beautiful sunset. The fish in the channel seemed more active than usual, in harmony with the evening concert of creatures and insects. All for my benefit, I believed.

The story of what happened in our little town became headline news. The drama drew national attention when the FBI began making arrests nationwide. It seems that Seth Russell was a small part of a large operation, explaining his ability to avoid detection. In fact, Seth Russell wasn't even his real name. Changing identities for every new job kept many of the organization's operatives under the radar, but I suspect Seth's ego floated his belief that it wasn't necessary. The Kaiti tattoos were a simple identification for those involved with him, and a mark of death for their executioner.

I didn't care about any of that. My sorrow came from

losing two fine police officers. One was a victim of circumstance, and the other, a young man with a promising future who made the wrong decision and chose to cross the line.

I'd just finished the last gulp of beer when I heard the front door unlock. I knew who had come to see me. She'd demanded a house key in case of an emergency.

"I figured I'd find you out here," Marty said.

I looked up to find her holding a grocery bag.

"I bought you some more beer and a few groceries." She pulled a can from inside the bag and handed it to me. "Take this. You look like you could use this."

"No argument here and thank you."

After a quick trip to the refrigerator, she pulled up a lounge chair.

"How are you feeling?"

"I'm sore, to be expected. Thank God for the man who invented Kevlar."

"How do you know it was a man?"

"Don't start with me, Marty. *I'm* still in recovery."

Her smile disappeared as quickly as it arrived. "Eldon, from now on, I think I'm going to be—"

My cell phone cut into her thought.

"I'm seriously considering getting rid of this thing," I grumbled, and checked the caller ID. "Oh no, it's Sam."

"Maybe he wants to apologize for being such a jerk during this whole thing."

"I doubt it." I turned off the phone, tossed it into the backyard, and took a sip of beer.

"So, Eldon, as I was saying, I think I'm going to be a little more wary of the guys I meet from now on."

"That's up to you, Marty, but selective might be a better position to take."

"You're right. If there's one thing I've learned, it's that guys…people aren't always who they seem to be."

I felt better about Marty. Felt better about myself as well. Releasing a deep sigh, I enjoyed another sip of beer.

"So, Eldon, since you're *still in recovery*, how about I cook you dinner? I bought some chicken, a couple of potatoes to bake, even some brussels sprouts."

"I'd like that, but before we fire up the grill, let's enjoy the sunset. Looks like it's going to be a beauty."

"Good idea."

She repositioned the lounge chair and laid back.

A red-orange sun sinking beneath the blue-green waters of the Gulf of Mexico brightened the pastel sky and signaled the end of another day.

ACKNOWLEDGMENT

Thanks to George Salter, Claire Kemp, Theresa R. Richardson, D. T. Bush, Sue Lloyd Davies, Patricia Grayson, Heloise Jones, Tom Horrigan, past and present members of the Gulfport Fiction Writers, David Mather and the Gulfport Public Library, Technical Advisors Rod Steckel and Ken Beaudoin, Alex Cameron, Dia and the wonderful folks at the Neptune Grill. Special thanks to Lynn Taylor, Steph Post, and Jeffery Hess for their guidance, support, and friendship. Many thanks to my dear friends, Mike O'Malley, John and Nancy Lamson, Al and Nancy Karnavacius, Rim Karnavacius and Michelle Rego, Charles Lyon, Jim and Debby Herden. And my grateful appreciation of my family for all those years of putting up with the urban hermit.

Stephen Burdick was born and raised in Florida. He is a retired civil servant currently living in the Tampa Bay area. He enjoys getting together with friends and attending various events.

BOOKS

On the following pages are a few
more great titles from the
Down & Out Books publishing family.

For a complete list of books and to
sign up for our newsletter,
go to **DownAndOutBooks.com**.

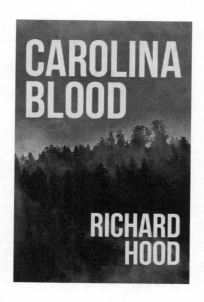

Carolina Blood
Richard Hood

Down & Out Books
August 2020
978-1-64396-146-0

When his well-to-do physician-father dies, James Thorwait discovers an old, back-room contract indicating that he is, in fact, an adopted child, whose parentage includes a mother named Allie Morelock, from far-back in the mountains of Western North Carolina.

Having grown-up in the rarified atmosphere of the well-born of Roalton, Tennessee, Thorwait must now confront the fact of his birth-mother's Appalachian heritage—and he goes in search of her, and her meaning.

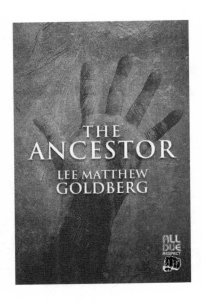

The Ancestor
Lee Matthew Goldberg

All Due Respect, an imprint of
Down & Out Books
August 2020
978-1-64396-114-9

A man wakes up in the Alaskan wilderness with no memory of who he is, except for the belief that he's was a prospector from the Gold Rush and has been frozen in ice for over a hundred years.

A meditation on love lost and unfulfilled dreams, *The Ancestor* is a thrilling page-turner in present day Alaska and a historical adventure about the perilous Gold Rush expeditions where prospectors left behind their lives for the promise of hope and a better future.

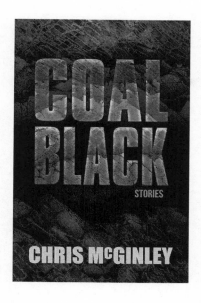

Coal Black: Stories
Chris McGinley

Shotgun Honey, an imprint of
Down & Out Books
December 2019
978-1-64396-058-6

Set in the hills of eastern Kentucky, these tales lay bare the dark realities of the region. Sometimes the backdrop is the opioid epidemic and all the human detritus and bloodshed that comes with it. Other times it's poachers or petty thieves who take center stage, people whose wild desperation invite danger everywhere they go. High in the hills the action takes place, alongside the rarely seen animals who hunt up there, and sometimes alongside the "haints" and spirits of popular folklore.

Coal Black is a collection of gritty crime stories—cleverly drawn tales with sometimes savage surprise endings.

Some Awful Cunning
Joe Ricker

Down & Out Books
April 2020
978-1-64396-086-9

Ryan Carpenter is an underground relocation specialist who helps people escape the danger and traumas of their life and start over. After agreeing to help the young wife of a Texas oil baron relocate her stepson to escape criminal prosecution, Ryan learns more than he wants to about the oil baron, his wife, and the stepson.

Haunted by his own forced relocation, Ryan betrays his client and is forced to scramble for his life, which only puts him face to face with the childhood past he's been trying to escape his entire life.

Made in the USA
Columbia, SC
01 May 2022

59554430R00112